IN HER SHOES

Probationer Nurse Katherine Cook is enjoying nursing until her friend, Annette, does something stupid . . . but it is Katherine who is accused of breaking a hospital rule by an unpleasant patient. Determined to protect Annette, Katherine refuses to betray her. Jack, the hospital porter, notices she is worried and offers to help. Katherine is delighted — until she finds his mother is not friendly, and Jack is not all he seems to be . . .

ANNE HOLMAN

IN HER SHOES

Complete and Unabridged

LINFORD
Leicester

First published in Great Britain in 2010

First Linford Edition
published 2012

British Library CIP Data

Holman, Anne, *1934 –*
 In her shoes.- -(Linford romance library)
 1. Nurses- -Fiction. 2. Love stories.
 3. Large type books.
 I. Title II. Series
 823.9′2–dc23

 ISBN 978–1–4448–0992–3

Published by
F. A. Thorpe (Publishing)
Anstey, Leicestershire

Set by Words & Graphics Ltd.
Anstey, Leicestershire
Printed and bound in Great Britain by
T. J. International Ltd., Padstow, Cornwall

Who's To Blame?

'Fire!' Probationer Nurse Katherine Cook yelled as she ran along the hospital corridor to sound the fire bell and to get a fire extinguisher.

She'd noticed smoke creeping from under the linen room door and, opening it, she'd seen bright flames licking around the piles of sheets and pillowcases, like a tongue devouring ice-cream. Coughing as the wooden slats in the linen room began to burn, she knew she couldn't smother it.

'Where's the fire, Nurse Cook?' a ward sister called. Dressed in her white starched cap and navy dress, she came bustling out of her ward to investigate.

With a shaking finger, Katherine pointed back down the corridor.

'Back there, in the linen cupboard, Sister.'

The older nurse kept her professional calm.

'I expect the firemen will be here soon. Come and help me to get the patients out of the fire exit. And reassure anyone that the fire engine will be on its way.'

In what seemed like a short time to Katherine, the patients were outside, and firemen had come and were dousing the fire with enough water to fill a swimming-pool.

By the time the Stamford Hospital Matron had come hurrying over from her office, she was informed that the fire was out and that no-one had been hurt.

The doctors, nurses and patients breathed more easily. Patients were escorted back to their beds. And the long job of mopping up began.

Afterwards, as the tired staff sat down to rest, chatting excitedly about the emergency, Katherine suddenly noticed her best friend, Probationer Nurse Annette Turney, was missing.

Finishing her cup of tea, Katherine went to look for her.

* ★ *

'Annette!' Katherine called in the nurses' cloakroom, where scarlet-lined navy cloaks hanging from pegs at first hid the young nurse.

'I'm over here, Katherine,' a muffled voice came from a corner of the room.

Katherine soon noticed the girl sitting huddled on the bench, her eyes sore from crying.

'What's the matter?' Katherine asked, sitting down beside her. She put her arm around her shoulders.

Katherine knew nursing had its happy times, but it also had sad moments, when young nurses felt they had to creep away and cry. It was only later in their career that they learned to cope with the heartache they sometimes felt looking after sick people.

Annette's hankie was a screwed-up

sodden ball in her hand as she wiped her eyes.

'Katherine,' she said in a husky voice, 'I think I may have started the fire. I was smoking in the linen cupboard, and . . . ' her voice dropped to a whisper, 'I panicked when I heard Sister calling me. I'm afraid I may not have stubbed out my cigarette properly.'

Aghast, Katherine looked at her friend with widened eyes, unable to think of anything helpful to say. She knew Annette smoked, as some nurses did, when she was off duty. But smoking on duty was breaking the rules of the hospital.

Annette was crazy to have done it. And in the linen room where flammable sheets, pillow cases, and towels were stored!

'Oh, Annette, how could you be so stupid!'

Annette gave another little sob and, breathing heavily, continued, 'I know I shouldn't have been smoking. I ought to go to Matron and tell her. But I'm afraid she will dismiss me if I do.'

Matron was a formidable woman and both girls knew it.

Katherine looked sorrowfully at her distressed friend as her slender body rocked backwards and forwards in grief. Annette had suffered from polio as a child and was not physically strong.

She'd missed out some of her schooling because of her illness, and Katherine was helping her with her nursing studies. Annette's older parents would be distraught if Annette was sent away from the hospital. Like Katherine — and strangely enough they did look alike, having neat figures and the same coloured hair — she was learning to become a good nurse.

It was just a shame Annette had disobeyed a hospital rule by smoking where, and when, she should not have been.

'You think I've been an idiot, don't you?' Annette sniffed as her red eyes looked at Katherine. 'I was so upset after having to assist Sister with a painful treatment the doctor had prescribed for a patient, and I needed to calm down. I thought a cigarette would help . . . ' She continued to sob for awhile then gulped, 'Now I feel like a coward, not owning up.'

Katherine sat wondering what advice to suggest. Then she shook her head, making her curls bounce under her nurse's cap.

Katherine said firmly, 'You were wrong to smoke on duty. Unlucky, too, because I know you are not normally a careless person — and I'm sure you would have put out your cigarette end carefully. I think it must have been someone else . . . '

'I always make sure my cigarette is put out — but, perhaps, this time I didn't?' Annette gave a gasp of anguish as fresh tears filled her eyes.

Katherine stood up and walked slowly to the window. She looked out at the big hospital. Medical advances in the treatment of the sick had made changing the original Infirmary buildings necessary.

The old Fever Blocks had been

altered into modern treatment wards, and now the war was over the hospital was being filled with sophisticated equipment.

Extensions were being added. Increasing numbers of house doctors and consultants needed room to provide specialist care. Katherine found it exciting to see improvements being made for curing patients. She loved nursing, and knew Annette did, too.

She couldn't bear the thought that Annette might be sent away for breaking a hospital rule, and possibly causing a fire. And Katherine might be sent away, too, if she didn't report Annette.

But would anyone know if they did not?

'I think no good will come of it even if you own up now, Annette. The fire has been put out and no great harm's been done. And we don't know for sure who started the fire. Anyway, Matron is short of nurses at this time just after the war, so she wouldn't want to lose two probationers because of a genuine mistake . . . '

'I promise I won't smoke ever again,' Annette declared.

'Good for you!' Katherine said, giving her friend an encouraging smile. 'Now we'd better get back to our wards before we're missed.'

* * *

Later that day, when all was back to the normal orderliness Matron insisted on in her hospital, Nurse Cook was standing before Matron trying not to look as though she was shivering in her shoes. Katherine, not wanting to tell Matron it was Annette who had been smoking in the linen room, said she thought it was a patient who was the culprit.

Matron's glasses flashed as she asked Katherine, 'Who was the patient you saw smoking, Nurse Cook?'

'I don't know who it was, Matron.' Crimson-faced Katherine felt uncomfortable as she looked down at the floor, determined not to inform on her friend.

Matron looked at her young nurse keenly. Katherine had been near the fire and had set off the fire alarm, which made Matron question her.

'Very well.' Matron's narrowed eyes looked suspiciously at the young nurse. 'As no significant damage occurred, I will say no more. However . . . ' she continued, 'should you remember anything about the incident, you are to come and tell me.'

'Yes, Matron.'

Watching Matron stalk away like a cock fluffed up in her decorative cap and distinctive navy and white uniform, Katherine gave a sigh of relief.

Katherine went to find Annette to tell her what Matron had said.

Annette was cleaning bed pans in the sluice.

Katherine whispered, 'I wonder if Matron thinks I know more about the incident than I told her. She will be after me if I do the slightest thing wrong now.'

'Thank you, Katherine,' Annette mumbled as she wiped a tear from her cheek. 'I don't see why Matron should suspect you of being involved. I'm the one at fault. Anyway, I've learned a hard lesson and I'll keep my promise not to smoke ever again.'

Katherine, never one for being down for too long, smiled at her friend and Annette's face lit up, too, as Katherine went on to say, 'That's one good thing that's come out of the fire. Now you'll have more money to enjoy for other things.'

The pittance young pupil nurses earned was only enough to keep them in stockings, which laddered too easily, and very little else. Even the local cinema manager offered nurses free tickets to enable them to have some occasional entertainment to relieve their hard work.

★　★　★

Only one person, a male patient, walking from his bed to the toilet, had observed a nurse light up a cigarette as the linen room door was *ajar*. *He'd noticed* her slip away and thought it was Nurse Cook, although it was her friend, Nurse Turney, because they looked very similar in uniform.

Furtively, he'd gone in the linen room after her for a smoke — until he'd heard someone coming, and he'd quickly returned to his ward.

It was his burning cigarette stub that in his haste had not been properly put out. Smouldering on the shelf where he'd left it, it soon set fire to a pile of towels.

The patient was Gerry Mitchell, who was recovering from an appendectomy. He was a short man with wide shoulders, who thought too well of himself. He really liked pretty Nurse Cook. But, knowing she did not show any interest in him, he planned to hint he might tell the matron about her smoking in the linen room — if she did not agree to go out with him.

In the nurses' dining room the next

day, when the nurses who where about to go on duty were given information, Katherine learned that she was assigned to the ward where Gerry Mitchell was.

The stocky man was sitting up in bed, grinning confidently as she went with a staff nurse to supervise his medicine and treatment.

'Good morning, Mr Mitchell,' the staff nurse said. 'I'm going to watch Nurse Cook dress your wound this morning. Draw the curtains, please, Nurse.'

'She's a learner, ain't she?'

The nurse retorted, 'Nurse Cook is the best nurse in the second year set, Mr Mitchell. All nurses have to learn nursing skills.'

'On the best patients, eh?'

'Exactly.' She laughed.

Katherine didn't chuckle, though. She knew Gerry Mitchell looked unpleasantly assured, leering at her. And he was enjoying her discomfort as she fumbled with the simple task of changing the dressing.

'Nurse Cook needs a smoke to calm her nerves,' Gerry quipped with a twisted grin.

Katherine's face flamed. She wanted to retort she didn't smoke, but she realised if she did then she might be letting Gerry know which nurses did. It was better she remained silent and concentrated on her task.

'You're all butterfingers today, Nurse Cook!' the staff nurse exclaimed. 'Although, as usual, I can't fault your work.'

'She hurt me,' Gerry said accusingly, making poor Katherine blush even more and dislike him for making her feel so nervous.

'I dare say you'll live,' the nurse replied briskly. 'Your wound is healing nicely, Mr Mitchell. Now I must go and attend to another patient. I'll leave Nurse Cook to tidy up here,' she said before, swishing the curtain aside, she marched off down the ward, leaving Katherine with Gerry.

Gerry tried to take her hand, but

Katherine was quick enough to pick up the soiled dressings and scissors, putting them in a kidney dish before he caught her.

'Hard to get, eh, Nurse? Never mind, I've got plenty of time for you to repay me for keeping my mouth shut, ain't I?'

'What do you mean?' Katherine asked, alarmed.

'I know who started the fire yesterday, don't I?'

Katherine gulped. Maybe he did.

'Mind you, I'll keep quiet. Especially if you come to the pub with me for a drink when I get out of this place.'

Horrified that he was enjoying tormenting her, Katherine felt sick.

She was in a dilemma. Gerry was accusing her for smoking where she shouldn't have been, but she didn't want to say it was her friend, not her, he must have caught sight of.

So Katherine pressed her lips together tightly. As she cleared away the soiled dressings she stubbornly refused to be persuaded into going out with a man she disliked.

She was thankful a day later when Gerry Mitchell was discharged, and she would no longer be pestered by him for a date.

Jack Cares For Katherine

Katherine was relaxing in the Nurses' Home lounge, having finished an arduous day's shift, when she was called to the phone.

Going out into the lobby she picked up the receiver.

It was a man's voice. Katherine struggled to think who it might be as he said, 'Hello, Nurse Cook, or should I call you Katherine, as you are off duty?'

'Hello,' she said cautiously. 'Who are you?'

'It's Gerry Mitchell here.'

Almost dropping the receiver in fright at hearing his brash voice, Katherine replied, 'Well, Mr Mitchell, I hope you are feeling better now you are at home — '

'I will be — if you would meet me for a drink tonight.'

Alarmed, she replied quickly, 'I'm sorry, I can't. I've just come off duty and need an early night because I start work at seven tomorrow morning.'

'Tomorrow, then?'

'No, thank you. I have . . . another important — '

Gerry laughed unpleasantly.

'Important, Nurse? What is more important than me not telling tales about you smoking where you did? And what a burn-up that caused!'

His chortle made Katherine's toes curl in her shoes. He was tormenting her!

The phone was in the Nursing Home lobby and there was little privacy for private conversations.

Nurse Katherine Cook was quite capable of telling the horrid man what she thought of him and his insinuating remarks . . . but dare she say anything that someone might overhear and question her about?

Desperate to think of something to shake him off, as many nurses were

17

standing nearby waiting to use the phone, Katherine replied, 'Maybe another time.'

'On your day off?'

'You'll have to wait for a while. I'm starting night duty next week. Goodbye.'

Her hands were shaking when she put the receiver down. Having put him off she knew it was only a matter of time before he cornered her again.

She gasped for breath. It was a worry to know what to do.

She didn't want to meet him. She didn't want to have anything to do with Gerry Mitchell.

Apart from anything else, the Gerry Mitchell situation was annoying, especially as Katherine was hoping the porter, Jack Holt, might ask her out. And she did genuinely like him. But Jack was popular with the other nurses and Katherine had the feeling he already had a girlfriend because he was never around when he went off duty.

Perhaps he lived in a nearby village

and went off there on his bike? He never went to the hospital socials or dances.

However, the handsome porter had noticed her change of spirits.

Next morning, after he'd helped wheel a patient back into the ward after surgery and the ward sister had taken charge of the patient, he was rolling the trolley back towards the lift and seeing her, he stopped.

'What's up, Nurse? You look down in the dumps. And that's not like you.'

Katherine, who was running down the hospital stairs to collect some medicine from the pharmacy for a patient, stopped as she heard the porter call her.

She'd noticed before that he was kindly-looking, and always well-mannered. It had struck her that he was a man who should be a doctor rather than a porter — but there you are, she thought, you couldn't always judge a person by their appearance.

'I'm very well, thank you,' she

answered. 'And yourself?'

He came nearer, seeming to analyse her, and saying, 'I detect something is bothering you, Nurse Cook.'

She gave a quick chuckle.

'Oh, certainly. I'm on night duty next week, I have a ladder in the only pair of black stockings I possess at present, and I don't get paid until the end of the month. My nursing examinations are coming up in a couple of months and I haven't revised properly yet. Oh, and I'm late collecting the medicine I've been told to get. Now, Mr Porter, have I given you enough symptoms?'

'More than enough!' Jack laughed.

'I must get on,' Katherine said, continuing walking downstairs, but she looked up at Jack who was leaning over the banister.

'Take care,' he called.

'Do you really care?' She stopped to question him.

'Indeed I do, Nurse Cook. I'm keeping an eye on you.' His smile seemed genuine, his voice warm and sincere. 'You need someone to keep a brotherly eye on you.'

Katherine wasn't sure a brotherly eye was enough. But she called back, 'You can keep an eye on me if you wish — but it will be difficult because I'm never in the same place for long — and neither are you.'

'You — and your beautiful smile — are always on my mind,' he called back.

Katherine was surprised he told her he often thought about her — as she did about him. It was comforting at a time when her worries were building up.

Not that she expected a porter to be able to help her!

Reaching the bottom step she turned her eyes upwards again. He was still watching her.

She wondered if he was seriously interested in her, with so many attractive nurses at the hospital for him to choose from. Not that she had ever heard or seen that he was going out with any of them.

It would be wonderful for her to be able to tell him about her problem. She didn't want to worry her mum, and she wondered what advice Jack would give her.

Would he go straight to Matron with the information that her friend had been reckless? No, she didn't think he would do that.

Could she trust him?

Anyway, as she walked briskly along the hospital corridor she thought she would never get the chance to discuss the problem with Jack and had better concentrate on her nursing duties.

* * *

Nursing was exhausting work, even without having to take exams. Katherine was feeling more dragged down with her worries every day. And tired, too — especially when Annette wanted her to go home with her on her day off so that they could revise together for their coming examinations.

'I'm hopeless at exams,' Annette moaned. 'You are brilliant at learning the work, Katherine. And if we work together we could practise some of the practical nursing skills we might be asked to perform.'

'OK, after my spell of night duty is over,' Katherine agreed, feeling reluctant to have to spend her precious time off helping Annette, yet knowing her friend badly needed her guidance.

On night duty for the next two months there was only time to work, sleep and eat. Besides, nurses only got one day off a week. And it was enough for her to get through her own nursing examination work — without having to help Annette pass exams, too. But she knew Annette lacked confidence, and sometimes it was her nervousness that was the cause of her low marks.

In Katherine's opinion, Annette would be a valuable qualified nurse in the hospital if she managed to pass her examinations to become a State Registered Nurse.

'You are kind,' Annette said. 'Thank you. Some day I hope I'll be able to help you in some way.'

'Perhaps you will,' Katherine replied, unconvinced she ever would. And yet, she reflected, you never know. Sometime she might be glad of a little help from her friend, so she added, 'Thanks, Annette.'

Although Katherine kindly agreed to help her friend, she regretted having so little time away from nursing. She needed to visit her mother and have some fun. In fact, she had a hobby — she collected shoes!

★ ★ ★

'Kitty, love, what are you doing?'

'Dusting my shoes, Mum.'

Mrs Margaret Cook always called her daughter, Kitty. She frowned, thinking her daughter had far too many shoes — especially for a nurse who wore flat-heeled, laced-up shoes for work each day.

Going upstairs she heard her humming the popular song, 'You broke my heart a million ways when you stole my happy days and left me lonely nights . . . '

'Kitty, you shouldn't be buying so many shoes!'

'Mum, you know I have just enough pay to buy the black stockings I have to wear at the hospital, so I can't afford to buy new shoes. Anyway, the shoes the shops sell are mostly utility ones. I find pre-war shoes that I like. People give them to me, or I buy them at auctions for next to nothing.'

'I think they are horrid old shoes!'

'No, they are not! We'll never agree on my shoe collection. I always select the shoes I acquire very carefully.

'Before the war, ladies' clothes were elegant and they had beautifully made shoes. When I put on some of my evening shoes they make me feel like a lady dancing the night away.'

Margaret sighed.

'You'll never find a man who'll want to marry a girl with a heap of old shoes!'

'If you were in my work shoes all day, you'd be glad to have a choice of attractive ones to wear after work.'

'Kitty, I shall never understand your liking for them.'

'Ah, but you're not in my shoes.'

If she were, she would understand why her daughter she called Kitty, hated being called Kitty.

She was told it had been her doting grandfather who'd nick-named her Kitty when she was a gurgling, curly-headed baby lying in her cot. And so her family called her Kitty, and she'd been stuck with that name all through her childhood.

Her father, a soldier who'd died at Dunkirk at the beginning of the war, she couldn't remember, but she thought he'd probably called her Kitty as a baby.

Katherine didn't want to upset her mum by insisting on changing her name.

Her mother was a kindly person and Katherine thought she'd managed well, bringing her up without the support of her father, and she didn't like to make her mother change her ways.

But in 1948, when she was grown up, she enrolled for nursing training and she told them her name was Miss Katherine Cook.

So Kitty Cook was left behind at home. Everyone at the hospital called her Nurse Katherine Cook.

However, two names could be awkward at times.

Recently, a patient who knew her mum, was admitted into the ward where Katherine was working.

'Why, Kitty, I didn't know you were a nurse. I thought you worked in a shoe shop in town?'

'Hello, Mrs Blackwell.' Katherine smiled as she came up to the older lady. 'Yes, I did for a while, now I'm in my second year of nursing training.' She pointed to her epaulettes, which showed her hospital nursing rank.

'Do you like nursing, my dear?'

'I do. Very much. Now I'm going to draw the curtains so you can change into your nightie and pop into bed. The house doctor will be around soon to examine you.'

'It's lovely to have you here, Kitty, nursing me.'

'I'm not on the wards all the time. Some mornings I have to attend Nursing School.'

'I'll be sure to tell your mum how sweet you look in your nurse's uniform, Kitty.'

'Mrs Blackwell, I, er, want to tell you that, here in the hospital, they call me by my real name, Katherine.'

'Oh,' Mrs Blackwell said, surprised. 'I'll try and remember that.'

I hope you will, Katherine thought. Some people can be forgetful. And Mum might be upset that I have changed my name without consulting her.

But, after the fire, that was the least of her worries. Katherine had just seen the duty roster and found that she was starting night duty for a spell on Monday. That was always difficult to get used to — being up when everyone else was in bed asleep.

But one good thing would come of it and that was that Gerry Mitchell would not be able to ask her out. As a night nurse she had a busy time, and after work there was no time for a social life.

By the end of her spell of night duty Gerry Mitchell would have found himself another girlfriend, and would have forgotten all about her.

She hoped.

The Right Career

Katherine felt inspired after hearing in class about the history of Stamford Hospital from one of the surgeons. He reminded the nurses of the early days when there was no hospital for the poor and sick, and because a rich citizen of Stamford left money in his will, and many others raised money by organising charities, balls, fêtes and markets, there were enough funds to build the Infirmary, as it was called in those days.

'And a brew house,' the lecturer said, 'because the first patients in 1828 were allowed one-and-a-half pints of beer a day.'

During the nurses' laughter, Katherine whispered to Annette, 'I wish the brew house was still here. I could do with a drink.'

But when the surgeon went on to tell

them about some of the first rules and orders of the hospital, the nurses nodded their heads and thought that they would not have liked some of those early regulations he described.

'I for one,' the speaker said, 'would not be here, because anyone over fifty years old was not hired!'

Trying to stifle their giggles, the nurses did not want to embarrass the speaker, who was giving them such an interesting talk and making them proud of their profession.

'Many people have devoted their working lives to this institution,' he ended his talk by saying. 'And you are the cream of the cream. Modern nursing has been built, like the hospital itself, not only on the kindness of donors, but by the skill of the medical profession, and the constant search for improvement in medicine — of which you are now a part.'

'Well,' Katherine said after the clapping had died down, 'that makes us feel we have chosen the right career, doesn't it, Annette?'

'Yes, it does,' she agreed.

But as they left class, Katherine was thoughtful. Should she tell Annette about Gerry Mitchell pestering her?

She really didn't want to burden Annette with that worry. The young nurse was worried enough about passing her nursing exams, which were difficult for her.

I must talk to someone, Katherine realised. She was becoming tense and tired, and she wasn't sleeping well — all signs of being under stress. And sooner or later she would . . . oh dear, she dreaded to think what might happen if she was not careful. She might make a mistake, or have an accident . . .

One of the senior nurses might report her to Matron for not being as competent as she should be. And Matron would be sure to question her — and could she avoid telling Matron what was upsetting her?

Katherine stood wondering what she should do as Annette walked away towards the ward she was on.

Standing in a trance after all the nurses had hurried off to their wards, she was aware that Jack, the good-looking porter, was pushing an empty wheelchair towards her.

'Want a lift, Nurse?' he called to her in his usual jocular manner.

'Not that kind of a lift, thank you. I am just about capable of walking at present. But I don't know for how long,' she replied tiredly, with a sigh.

He was near her now, searching her eyes and looking worried about her.

Perhaps she ought to tell the porter about her troubles? He seemed a sensible man, and he might be able to suggest what she should do.

She blurted out, 'What would you do if someone was . . . harassing you?'

He raised an eyebrow looking at her thoughtfully.

Katherine swung around and began walking away from him down the corridor.

'Hey! Stop, Nurse.' He'd left the

wheelchair and his quick strides soon caught up with her. Laying his hand gently on her shoulder he said quietly, 'We need to talk about this.'

Halting, Katherine felt somewhat comforted. He was showing sympathy. She couldn't be rude and brush him off.

'I don't know what you can do about it,' she retorted.

'Two heads are better than one,' he replied seriously.

Katherine pressed her lips together and looked down at the floor.

'I don't want to pry into your business, Nurse. But I've noticed something has been bothering you for far too long. If I can help you, I'd be glad to. But I can't unless you tell me what it's all about, can I?'

'Well, it involves someone else. I can't tell you without betraying a confidence.'

'You'll have to trust me.'

She looked up at him and wondered.

He had pleasing features, manners like a doctor, and seemed willing to listen. He added in his baritone voice, 'I think you shouldn't be bottling all this up inside. Whatever is bothering you should be let out.'

Katherine's teeth clenched. Could she trust him? He seemed anxious to listen to her woes. And she couldn't think of anyone else who might help her.

Besides, she'd already admitted she had a problem concerning being harassed, so she might as well tell him all about it.

They agreed to meet at a good village pub the next day and have a meal, which he kindly agreed to pay for — and she didn't argue about that!

★ ★ ★

The following day she was amazed when Jack drove up to the The Falcon Inn in a classy sports car — not on the bicycle he normally rode to work.

She was sitting waiting for him on one of the benches outside the pub and watched him get out of his car — she was amazed again.

He was wearing smart casual clothes.

Of course he wouldn't come in his porter's uniform, she chided herself. But he did look surprisingly like a professional man.

'Ah, there you are,' he said with a smile that melted her tension as he strode towards her. 'I'm sorry to keep you waiting.'

Katherine looked at her watch.

'You haven't. I had to catch the bus that got here twenty minutes early.'

'I'll get you a drink. What would you like?'

She asked for a fruit drink, and again, to her surprise, he said he would have a non-alcoholic drink, too.

There is something mysterious about Jack, she mused. I'm learning as much about him as he will learn about me. He certainly didn't appear to be short of cash as she was. His income as a porter would not be great. Perhaps he had another job? Or his family might be well off.

He suggested, 'As it's a pleasant summer evening, shall we sit outside?'

'Why not?'

'OK then, you choose a table while I get the drinks.'

She looked around for a quiet spot under a willow tree for shade, and close to the river so they could watch the moving water stream under the bridge.

When he returned, it didn't take long for Katherine to tell him with complete honesty all she'd been worried about. Listening, without interrupting her, he nodded and took a sip of his drink every now and again.

'Well,' he said, after she'd admitted telling Matron it was a patient who'd started the fire, 'you didn't light a cigarette in the linen room. Nurse Annette Turney told you she did, and may not have put it out — although it could well have been a patient. You've been protecting a friend.' He took a sip of his drink and added, 'A fine thing to do.'

'I suppose you're right.'

She looked at Jack's serious expression and knew he was not just making an excuse for Annette. He was trying to understand what really happened.

'Now the other thing that strikes me,' he continued, 'is that the patient, Gerry Mitchell, is untrustworthy. Even I, as a porter, get to know something about the patients. And what I've heard about him makes me think I wouldn't trust him an inch. He's a smoker, and more likely to have started the fire himself and wanted to blame someone else.

'He may have seen Nurse Turney smoking and thought it was you. Now he is trying to pressurise you into going out with him — which is despicable!'

'Ah,' Katherine exclaimed, 'so you think I am right to avoid him?'

'Certainly I do!' He paused for a moment, looking at her with compassion in his eyes. 'I would go further than that. I think you must keep well away from him.'

They sat in silence for a while,

looking towards the river and the quacking, fast swimming ducks as they snapped up some bread from a sandwich a lady and a child were throwing into the water for them.

'How can I?' Katherine asked, looking at him intently.

'How can you what?' Jack replied.

'Sorry, my mind was far away. Watching the ducks. I love ducks.'

Jack smiled.

'I do, too.'

Katherine gathered her thoughts. It had been easy to talk to Jack. She felt comforted to think he now knew of the fix she was in.

But, of course, the problem remained.

'I mean, how can I avoid being asked out by Gerry Mitchell?'

Jack cleared his throat.

'Well . . . you could start coming out with me?' His raised eyebrow was most appealing.

Pinkness coloured Katherine's cheeks.

'Yes,' she said. 'I could.' She dare not look at him now. It was her dream come true that he was asking her out. She said, 'I don't want you to take me out because you feel sorry for me.'

He chuckled.

'I was already planning to ask you out, Katherine.'

It was the first time he had used her first name, and she liked the way he said it. But was it true he was attracted to her, as she was attracted to him? Or was he just feeling sorry for her?

He finished his drink and said, 'It's simple. If you're my girl, and I am taking you out, Gerry Mitchell won't be able to, will he?'

Knowing she had little time off duty, she realised it would be one excuse she could use to avoid Gerry. And, thinking of the thrill of being Jack's girlfriend, she smiled excitedly at him.

'That's a good idea. But our days off may not always coincide.'

'Ah, well,' he said, sitting up straight and looking into her eyes, 'Now it is my turn to make a confession.'

Katherine blinked.

'Yes,' he said. 'I want you to know — but keep it under your hat. I'm only at the hospital temporarily. And I'm there on a voluntary basis. Because I am replacing another porter.'

What a shame he was not going to be staying at the hospital!

'Why? Don't you like the work?' she asked in a disappointed voice.

'I've got used to it. But it is not my career.'

Baffled, Katherine stared at him.

'Then, why . . . ?'

'Let me explain. I'm an accountant. Last year I was driving home one evening after work, and at a bend of the road I didn't see a cyclist who had no lights on his bike, and he was wearing dark clothes. I slammed on my brakes and tried to stop quickly as another car was approaching at speed. I only nudged the cyclist with my car, but the poor fellow was knocked off his bike and was injured.'

'Oh dear!'

'He was taken to hospital and

41

treated for multiple minor injuries. I discovered he was a porter there. So, to help him, I decided I would do his job and get his pay for him until he had recovered from the injuries I had given him.'

'Oh,' Katherine said. 'That was a fine thing to do!'

'I thought it was only fair. Anyway, it was about time I learned how the other half lived.'

She admired his honesty.

'But what about your accountancy work?'

'I work for myself, so there's no problem. I have time after I finish at the hospital to keep things ticking over. I'm not exactly on the breadline.'

She could well believe that. He struck her as being comfortably off. His car was not the cheapest.

'And what about your other girl-friends?' she asked a little fearfully.

'I have no special girlfriend at present. So may I ask you to fill the post?'

'If you truly want me to.'

'Yes, I do.'

Flattered, she replied, 'The other nurses will be jealous to hear that Jack, the handsome porter, has chosen me.'

He laughed.

'I'm the lucky one. I have caught the best nurse.'

'Not with the baggage of trouble I carry.'

He became serious.

'Not now, Katherine. Mr Mitchell will soon get the message to leave you alone.'

She felt a great relief — as well as being thrilled to think of going out with Jack. Then she glanced at her watch, saying, 'I must go. I'll miss the bus and have Matron after me for being late on duty.'

He got his car keys out of his pocket.

'I'll run you back,' he said, standing and pulling her garden chair back so that she could get up easily. Walking with him to the car, Katherine felt strangely elated, and after her misery, it seemed as if she was walking on air.

Driving back to the hospital Jack said, 'I'll give you my card. You can ring me at any time. I live with my mother.'

On the small white card he gave her was printed his address, telephone number, and his name. It said *Martin Holt*.

'Is your name, Jack or Martin?' she asked as the car swept into the hospital grounds.

'Either. Whatever you chose. Martin is my real name. I call myself Jack at the hospital. I know it's odd to have two names — '

'Not to me,' she said, 'I have two names, too. Katherine is my real name, but my family call me Kitty.'

'What shall I call you, then?'

'Katherine. Definitely.'

'Well, then, Katherine, I promise you I'll be available at any time if you should want me.'

She believed him and said, 'Thank you, Martin.'

She liked the name Martin. Martin Holt sounded dependable — and she felt sure he was.

Katherine was so relieved to feel she now had a shining knight to help her and she slept well for the first time in weeks. Her cheerful self returned.

★ ★ ★

One of Katherine's fellow nurses, Sylvia, nudged another nurse at breakfast the following day and remarked, 'Katherine went out yesterday and just look at her today. She's all smiles.'

Jean was curious.

'I wonder where she went?'

'She goes home with Annette sometimes — her mother lives not far away.'

Sylvia chuckled.

'From the look of her face, I'm sure she's been out with a man.'

'I didn't know she was courting anyone. So it must be a new boyfriend.'

'I wonder who it was.'

The two young nurses grinned at each other and looked over towards Katherine, who was humming to herself as she poured milk on her cornflakes. She was in a world of her own, thinking about the porter, Jack Holt, who she now knew as Martin Holt.

Jean whispered, 'I saw her talking to that cocky patient, Gerry Mitchell. He's been discharged, but perhaps he asked her out?'

'Could be. But unlikely, because that creep wouldn't bring sunshine into any girl's life. No, I have the feeling she's captured someone better — Jack the porter!'

'Wow! He's a catch. But good luck to her if she has. Katherine is a very nice girl, and an excellent nurse.'

Planning A Future

'Martin,' his mother said as they enjoyed their morning cup of coffee seated in her warm conservatory. 'Now that you are about to finish that porter's job you're doing at the hospital, I'm looking forward to you returning to being as you were before the accident.'

Martin sighed as he folded the business section of the newspaper and put it down on the side table beside the basket chair where he was sitting.

It was pleasant sitting in the sunny room, which led out into his mother's well-kept garden. She'd filled it with house plants that thrived in the glass-walled room, giving out an earthy aroma and fragrance from some of the flowering pot plants.

'Mother,' he said, looking at her as he leaned back and crossed his long legs,

'I've not quite finished the job there.'

'Oh?' Mrs Valerie Holt frowned. 'I thought you told me you were doing your last shift next week.'

Martin ran his fingers through his fringe as he thought of his promise to look after Katherine.

'That's true. But I've still got a few jobs to tidy up that might mean going back there occasionally.'

'Oh dear, I was hoping you were going to forget all about the hospital and become the carefree young man you were before that unfortunate accident.'

Martin retorted, 'I can't be. I've grown — learned a lot. Become a different person.'

Valerie bristled.

'But that's ridiculous! You can't change yourself.'

Martin smiled at his mother. 'Then let us say I've moved on. Lost some of my former interests, and taken on others. I'm planning my future.'

'Ah, now that is what I wanted to talk

to you about.' She smiled at him. 'Your future. It's about time you got married. Jilly Masters has been asking after you. She's such a lovely girl. And she's very fond of you.

'So I decided to invite her, and her mother, over for the weekend. So you and she could get to know each other better. And it'll be nice for me to have her mother, Joan, my old school friend, here, too.'

Martin groaned inwardly. It wasn't as if he disliked Jilly. She was a very nice girl. But he found it hard to talk to her.

She was in his opinion, a pretty, pleasant girl, but shallow. She had no interests other than shopping, dancing and having fun. Compared with Katherine, she seemed unexciting to be with.

Valerie continued, 'I've organised a theatre visit on Friday night, and a dinner party on Saturday, and we could all go to the botanical gardens after lunch on Sunday, so you young people can be together.'

Martin felt annoyed. He didn't want

to be tied down all the weekend in case Katherine was in trouble and wanted him.

'I known you mean well, but you should have consulted me. I can't promise to be there all the weekend.'

'Why ever not?'

Martin looked out over his mother's neatly manicured garden. It was an agreeable sight in the early summer weather. She was so good at organising it.

And he not only admired his mother's skilful gardening and housekeeping, she worked at keeping herself trim and well attired and he was proud of her.

Unfortunately, she liked to organise him, too.

He'd been thinking while he was working at the hospital, that since his father had died she'd persuaded him to live at home with her. And she mothered him too much.

He must leave her and live his own life. And he ought to start to make the break now.

'Mother,' he said firmly, 'as I explained, I've another engagement this weekend, I've promised to help someone, and I can't let them down.'

'Jilly will be disappointed if you keep hopping off all the time.'

'I haven't invited her here.'

'Jilly's not to know that! She'll think you are not interested in her.'

He wasn't. Besides, he didn't want his mother's choice of a bride for him. He said, 'You'll have to tell her I've other commitments.'

'It will seem bad-mannered.'

'Not if you say I'm needed at the hospital.'

She looked affronted.

'You used to be so available. Now you seem to want to rush out of the door.'

Martin adjusted his position placing his elbows on the chair arm rests and putting his fingertips together. He looked at his elegant mother and sighed.

He loved her and didn't want to hurt her. But for some time he'd recognised he needed to summon the courage to gain his independence from her.

He took a deep breath and said, 'I've been thinking, I've a lot of work to do in Stamford. I'm considering living there for a while, so I don't have to make the long journey over there every day.'

Martin was sorry to see that disappointment filled Valerie's eyes. It would be a wrench for a recently widowed lady like her.

She said, 'I doesn't take long to go from this village to Stamford by car.'

'True. But I'm particularly interested in a Stamford project and need to put in some extra hours — some evening work. Tom, a rugby friend of mine, lives there and I dare say I can bunk up with him for a while. I could do with the extra rugby training in the evenings, too. There are some big matches coming up this season.'

Valerie gave him startled look.

'I knew it. I knew when you got that crazy idea to work as a hospital porter after your accident that it would unsettle you. Why can't you just slip back into what you were always doing? You are comfortable here. You're making a good living.' She sighed. 'Besides, I like your company.'

Martin came and squatted down beside her chair, taking her hand.

'You know I'll have to leave you some time. You've just hinted that you would like me to consider Jilly as a future wife, haven't you?'

Valerie smiled.

'I would like some grandchildren,' she said wistfully.

'Well then, I must see about getting you some!' he said with a chuckle. 'But, you must allow me to chose my own wife.'

Valerie looked at him sharply.

'Jilly is suitable for you.'

Martin sprang up on to his feet. He strode to look at the wall cabinet which displayed his mother's collection of miniature shoes. She did what she wanted in life. She had her own hobby.

So he must stand up to what he wanted to do. He must be bold and tell her.

'I have another girl in mind,' he stated, turning around to face her. 'Although I'm not sure she's decided she wants me.'

Valerie sat up straight with shining eyes.

'Oh, that's marvellous! When can I meet her?'

Martin hesitated before he thought of an answer, knowing what she meant — when can I see her, to approve of her? His mother would be keen to find out if Katherine was acceptable in her eyes. But Katherine had enough problems to cope with at present without having to be checked over by his mother. Although, he couldn't see why they wouldn't get on.

He said, 'It's early days. She's in a bit of a fix just now and I want to help her out.'

She looked at him askance.

'You haven't got her into trouble, have you?'

'No! The trouble she has concerns another bloke.'

Valerie sounded disappointed when she asked, 'Is she a flighty type of girl?'

'Not at all. She's a loyal, hard-working nurse. Although she enjoys lots of things most girls do. Now, I must get off to the hospital.'

He could tell his mother was stunned to learn of him taking another girl out — especially one she had never met. She realised he'd have met lots of nurses working at the hospital and was lost for words.

As he left the conservatory she called after him.

'What shall I say to Joan and Jilly?'

He came back and stood at the conservatory door tapping his fingers on the door frame.

'Say I'm looking forward to seeing them. But explain that I have still some obligations at the hospital to fulfil and I might be unable to be with you all the time at the weekend.'

'Make sure you are here to escort us

to the theatre. And the dinner party. And for the visit to the botanical gardens.'

'I'll do my best.'

As Martin galloped up the stairs two at a time to get changed he muttered, 'And tell them three women against one man makes an uneven fight!'

But he was pleased he'd made the first move towards independence.

★　★　★

Katherine received a message on night duty to say that her mother had rung her.

Worrying her mother might be ill, she asked the ward sister if she could ring home and she was told she could, if she was quick about it.

'Mum, are you all right?'

'Yes, Kitty, I'm fine, love.'

'I'm not supposed to use the telephone at work in case there's an emergency. But the night sister said I could if I made the call short. So what is it you wanted?'

'There's a man been lurking around the house.'

Katherine thought of their quiet road lit with street lamps, with semi-detached houses each side and small front gardens. Why would anyone want to hang about there?

'Why don't you ring the police?' she suggested.

'I would . . . only, he hasn't done anything wrong.'

Katherine took some deep breaths.

'How long has he been there?'

'Well, I first noticed him standing on the pavement staring at the house about seven o'clock this evening, and then when I went up to bed I noticed he was still there as I drew the bedroom curtains.'

'What does he look like?'

'Difficult to say. He was wearing a dark jacket. He's gone now. I thought he might be waiting for you. A neighbour said he was looking for a girl called Katherine, so I wondered if it was you, Kitty.'

Had Gerry Mitchell found out where her mother lived?

Katherine knew she must ring off. She said desperately, 'Don't worry about it, Mum. But do ring the police and the local copper will keep an eye on the house when he's on his beat. Goodnight.'

Katherine had tried to sound as though she wasn't worried. But, of course, she was. Who could it be hanging about her mum's house?

Could it be Gerry Mitchell?

Or was it someone else?

She was most worried because he'd disturbed her mother.

Oh dear, how complicated her life had become because of that wretched fire. How she wished she had been honest and had not tried to protect Annette. No, that was not true. Of course she was right to help Annette.

* * *

Coming off night duty Katherine felt very tired, but she wanted to ring

Martin and ask his advice. Finding his card she rang his number.

She heard a lady's voice answering, 'Wansford, double five, seven.'

'Hello,' Katherine said. 'May I speak to Jack, please.'

'You have the wrong number,' Mrs Valerie Holt replied, irritated, because she was in bed and had been woken up at six o'clock in the morning.

Katherine said, 'I'm sure I have the right number.' Then she looked at the card again and corrected Jack, for Martin, saying, 'I mean, may I speak to Martin Holt, please.'

'Who are you? What do you want?'

It was none of her business, Katherine thought — although realising the lady was probably his mother, she replied, 'I'm a nurse at Stamford Hospital, and I would like to speak to him.'

Mrs Valerie Holt sighed. She thought this girl might be the nurse Martin said he was keen on. But the girl hadn't good manners — ringing at this very early hour in the morning and not saying why she wanted to speak to Martin.

This thoughtless nurse might replace her and Jilly in his affections, unravel her plans for her son.

Determined to put her off, Valerie said, 'Mr Holt is . . . away for the weekend.'

Katherine felt devastated. Martin had offered to help her and now he had gone away!

'May I leave a message for him?'

'Very well,' the lady huffed, sounding as if she was being asked to do a great favour. 'What is it?'

Ignoring her curtness, Katherine said, 'Please tell him Katherine rang.'

'Very well. Now, what is the message?'

'Nothing else. Just say Katherine rang.'

'Oh.' She sounded disappointed not to know why this nurse was ringing hoping to speak to her son. Valerie went on to say, 'Next time you ring, could you make it after eight in the morning?'

'Sorry,' Katherine said, 'I didn't realise ... I've just come off night duty.'

The lady just put the phone down.

Katherine felt tears come into her eyes.

Has Katherine Been Duped?

The next day Katherine awoke with a headache. And when one of the housemaids brought her in a cup of tea in bed, telling her, 'You'd better not be late for breakfast, I've been told Matron is coming over to the Nurse's Home to give out some information,' Katherine felt like burying her head under the blankets and staying there.

But, knowing there were some very sick patients needing her care, she sat up in bed and drank her tea, which revived her somewhat.

She thought about the man who had been hanging about her mother's house, and the fact that Martin Holt, despite his promise to help her, had gone away for the weekend!

She felt very let down.

Being a practical person, Katherine

tried to decide what to do. She hoped her mother had gone to the police about the snooping man. There could have been many reasons for a man to be waiting on the pavement outside the house.

As for Martin, well, she had been duped, hadn't she? Thinking he really cared for her. In a sense he'd been snooping, too. Wanting to find out what was bothering her, and after she'd told him, he hadn't taken it seriously.

Men could be like that. Fickle!

Anyway, Jack was no longer going to be around. He would be Martin Holt, accountant, from now on. And his life would be separate from hers.

Forget him, she told herself. But her whispering self kept telling her she couldn't.

She'd thought Martin really liked her, so she was disappointed. Angry, too, that she'd been caught up in this tangle, and all she had tried to do was help Annette.

Annette. Katherine remembered she'd promised to help Annette with her exams.

When her spell of night duty was over, instead of having a nice restful day, she'd promised to go over to Annette's bungalow and revise with her. And that was about the last thing she felt like doing.

But Katherine kept her promises — not like some people she knew!

The nurses on night duty ate their breakfast with the daytime nurses' who were having their dinner.

Katherine was sitting eating when two nurses spotted her. Sylvia and Jean came up and Jean said, 'An ex-patient, Mr Mitchell, came here yesterday asking after you.'

Katherine dropped her knife and fork with a clatter.

'Oh, no!'

Sylvia looked at Jean and said, 'Don't look so horrified. We didn't know if you were interested in him.'

'I'm not, I assure you!'

Sylvia remarked, 'He said you were.'

Katherine shouted in anger, 'Then he was lying!'

Sylvia and Jean looked at each other,

and Sylvia said, 'OK, there's no need to go off the deep end. We were surprised, we didn't think you would be friends with the likes of him, did we, Jean?'

Jean nodded in agreement.

'That's why we're asking you now,' Sylvia continued, 'in case he calls again.'

Katherine told them straight, 'I don't even like that man.'

Jean said, 'Sorry, we made a mistake.'

Katherine sat staring into space as the two nurses bustled off. What, she wondered, had Gerry asked the girls? Had he found out her home address? Had it been him loitering outside her mother's house?

It was all the more frustrating because she was tied up at the hospital and couldn't visit her mum. And Martin Holt, who was supposed to be helping her, had abandoned her like a sinking ship.

Pondering what she should do, she suddenly thought, maybe I could ask Annette to go and see my mum.

Annette had said she would do something for her if she could.

Katherine just managed to catch Annette going off duty.

Hurriedly she told her friend the problem.

'I'd be happy to visit your mother, Katherine. May I borrow your bike?'

'Of course. Ask Mum if that man has been around again. And ask her if she has been to the police as I suggested.'

'OK.'

Feeling happier that she had done all she could, Katherine went on night duty.

When the night shift was over, she saw a message — and a letter — waiting for her at the Nurses' Home. The message was from Annette to say her mother was fine, there had been no more sign of the man who'd been waiting outside the house and the police were keeping an eye on her house. That was a relief.

The envelope of the letter had neat handwriting. She tore it open to find it had been written by Martin Holt.

Dear Katherine,

My mother told me you rang, and I'm sorry I was out and I couldn't speak to you. I know you're on night duty just now and you'll not be able to go out to meet anyone at present. Let me know when you are free.

I'm making enquires about Mr Mitchell.

Take care,
Martin.

Katherine waved the letter in front of her face like a fan for awhile.

He'd gone off for the weekend and merely said he was sorry he was out. And then he asked her to let him know when she was free to meet him! Did he honestly expect her to ring and take another battering from that harridan of a mother of his?

And what was the point of writing to him if he was going to be away for weekends when it suited him? Finally, he'd written *take care*, as if he was concerned about the problem she had.

How did he imagine he was going to deal with it, when he'd left her to fend for herself?

And while Martin was enjoying his weekend, Gerry Mitchell was making himself a nuisance by questioning the nurses about her and hanging around her mother's house. So, what use were the 'enquires' he'd written he was making — what use was that?

Worst of all, she was devastated after she'd thought she could trust Martin, and found she could not. She'd naively thought he was going to be available when she needed him. It cut her deeply when she thought she loved him but couldn't depend on him.

Katherine put her palm to her forehead. She really didn't know whether it was Gerry Mitchell, or Martin Holt, who was causing her more grief.

However, being on night duty and well occupied, she was protected from both of them for a few weeks. She decided she would cast her worries aside for the present and concentrate on her nursing duties and revising for her coming exams. That would keep her busy.

And, hopefully, she would be able to think of a way of shaking them both off.

* * *

The next day she had off, Katherine went to Annette's home and they had a surprisingly hilarious time revising for their state exams.

Pretending to be the students' Sister Tutor, they mimicked her high voice and fussy manner, taking it in turns to ask each other questions and going over their lecture notes, as well as some practical work.

Kindly Mrs Turney had prepared a super lunch for them, and as Katherine enjoyed roast beef and Yorkshire pudding, she was told that Annette had admitted to her mother that Katherine was a wonderful friend to have kept quiet about her fear she may have started the hospital fire.

'Well, Mrs Turney,' Katherine said,

eyeing the delicious trifle she was about to eat next. 'I think Annette is a fine nurse, and deserves to be excused one careless mistake — if it was her fault. We don't know for certain that Annette's cigarette end did start the fire. It may well have been one of the patients — as I told Matron.'

'I've given up smoking now,' Annette said, 'so some good came from that disaster.'

'It would be marvellous if Annette passed her nursing exams,' her mother said, spooning the dessert into bowls.

'I'm sure she stands as good a chance as anyone in our set,' Katherine replied. 'She remembered some things this morning I had forgotten.'

Mrs Turney looked at her smiling daughter, saying, 'Dad and I were so worried about Annette when she was a child suffering from polio. She's battled hard to overcome her disadvantages. I pray she will be able to pass her exams. In fact, that you both become State Registered Nurses.'

Katherine looked at Annette and they both giggled, thinking they would indeed be proud to achieve that goal, which seemed a long way off with mountains of nursing work to do and difficult examinations to pass before they got there.

Also, Katherine knew she still had more than a few hurdles to overcome besides having tough hospital and state exams to pass before that happened.

'Katherine will pass her exams with ease,' Annette remarked, smiling at her. 'She always comes top of our class.'

'I'm not so sure about that,' Katherine said with a faraway look.

'Well,' Annette said, 'I know you've been worried of late . . . '

'Dear me,' Mrs Turney said, looking at Katherine with a concerned expression. 'What's been the matter, Katherine?'

'Oh, nothing much.' Katherine tried to sound dismissive.

Annette said, 'Some man was standing outside her mother's house, and it worried her.'

Mrs Turney said, 'Annette told me about that. It is unnerving to find some-one hanging about outside. But he could have been there waiting for someone or, knowing how pretty Nurse Katherine Cook is, he was probably an admirer!'

Katherine winced.

She didn't want to tell them about Gerry Mitchell wanting to take her out. Or the worst of it, that he was threatening her. So she said, 'My mother lives alone and can be a little sensitive about her property at times. Even a stray cat getting into her garden and frightening the birds can upset her.'

All three women smiled at each other.

Katherine said, 'Anyway, Mum told me that the man hasn't been back, and she mentioned it to the local bobby, so I hope she has forgotten all about it now. Anyway, thanks again, Annette, for going round to have a chat with her. I'm afraid she would have kept you for ages — Mum's a great chatterbox.'

'Your mum is a dear,' Annette said. 'I enjoyed talking to her. She calls you

Kitty, which amused me. She kept asking me questions about nursing and how we were getting on. And she mentioned your shoe collection. I never knew you collected shoes, Katherine. But I often wondered how you got hold of such pretty ones.'

'So did I,' Mrs Turney said. 'I didn't like to mention it, but the ones you have on now are lovely.'

'They're smashing!' Annette agreed, looking at them under the table.

Katherine blushed. She knew she had a weakness for shoes. And she had on a favourite pair of high heels in soft leather and peep-toes she'd found the last time she went to the auction room.

She'd bought them for next to nothing.

She never knew anyone noticed her shoes. She wondered if Martin had noticed what she wore when they went out together.

Why had she suddenly thought of him?

He was like a fly-by-night. Here today and gone tomorrow.

But Katherine knew in her heart that she couldn't cast Martin from her mind easily. She'd been deeply hurt thinking he really cared for her when he obviously didn't. But she was still attracted to him. She thought about him so much she might be in love with him.

'Anyway, Katherine,' Mrs Turney said, 'I know how much you have helped Annette, and her dad and I are so grateful to you. Now, please remember we are always here if you need any help from us at any time.'

'Thank you. Well, actually . . . ' Katherine said, as mother and daughter looked at her anxiously, 'I would appreciate a little more of your delicious trifle.'

They all laughed.

It had been an unexpected pleasant day, and it did Katherine good.

Gerry Mitchell Is Back

Having finished two months of night duty, and having resumed day shifts, Katherine had more time to think about Martin Holt who she couldn't seem to get out of her mind. As much as she had felt he had let her down, she still hankered after him and wanted to speak to him. So one day she decided to pluck up courage and rang his home again.

'May I speak to Mr Holt,' she said politely to the lady who answered the phone.

'Who's speaking?'

'A friend.'

Mrs Holt paused.

'I'm afraid he's not living here any more,' she said politely but flatly.

Katherine waited, hoping his mother would say where he'd moved to. But she didn't.

'Have you got his new telephone number?' Katherine asked.

'You could try ringing his office,' his mother said, crisply putting down the receiver.

She didn't have the chance to ask the name of his office. Or to suggest she asked Martin to ring her back.

It was clearly a put down. His mother probably knew it was the same nurse who'd rung him a few weeks ago. Nothing could have made it plainer to Katherine that his mother was trying to protect her son from her — or all girls who might be chasing him. It was, she thought, unfair. But Katherine gave a little shrug.

Her brief romance with Martin seemed to have come to an abrupt end.

Anyway, she wouldn't want a mother-in-law like Mrs Holt.

★ ★ ★

Katherine had been concentrating on swotting for her exams, and her mind was in a whirl. She badly needed a break.

It was her day off. And having a few items she needed to buy, she decided to go into town.

Hearing nothing from either men, she was dismayed that morning to see Gerry Mitchell waiting for her as she slipped out of the Nurses' Home to walk to the shops.

With a beating heart, Katherine gasped.

Gerry looked swanky because he was attired in the latest Teddy Boy fashion with a wide-shouldered long jacket and drainpipe trousers. His shoes had pointed toes and his long hair was greased up with a cheeky quiff.

Had she liked him, she might have given him credit for dressing in the latest expensive fashion for young men.

But, she not only disliked him — she felt slightly scared of him.

Propping himself up against a shiny Hillman car, he was casually smoking a cigarette.

He was obviously waiting for her, and immediately threw down his cigarette stub and squashed it into the pavement when he saw her.

There was no chance of her skipping past him. So Katherine turned to retreat quickly back into the Nurses' Home.

'Hey! Nurse Cook!' she heard him shout as his feet pounded after her.

She quickened her steps, hoping he dare not follow her into the grounds, but, alas, she might have known he would not be afraid to trespass.

He reached her before she got to the front door.

She muttered, 'I've forgotten my purse,' trying to skip past him. But he moved to prevent her.

Praying another nurse might come along, Katherine cried, 'Mr Mitchell, please let me past!'

Unfortunately there was no-one in sight, and Gerry knew it. His leering grin made her want to slap his face, but Katherine knew she was safely inside the Nurses' Home grounds and sooner or later someone would appear and she could ask them to help her.

She just had to keep calm and think of something that would release her from Gerry.

'What do you want?' she asked.

'You know what I want, Katherine. Like I said months ago, I want to take you out. I'll take you for a ride in my new car right now.'

She took a deep breath. Thinking fleetingly of what Martin had told her, that under no circumstances must she go out with Gerry Mitchell.

She said, 'Thank you, Mr Mitchell, but I can't go. I have things I must do before I go back on duty.' She side-stepped away from him, edging towards the steps that led up to the front door.

'You were going out,' he said accusingly.

Katherine glared at him.

'I was. But I remembered I'd forgotten my purse,' she fibbed. 'I need to go back for it.'

'You won't need any money. I've got plenty,' he said. Taking out his bulgy wallet, he showed her. He certainly had money to spend. But she thought he was showing off and that didn't impress her.

'I've forgotten to get my shopping list,' she replied, desperately trying to think of a way to get away from him.

He ignored her — or realised she was making an excuse to get away from him.

'Look, I've been waiting around for you for months. I've got us a flash new car here all ready for a spin — '

'I can't go now.'

'I'll continue to wait . . . believe me, I will.'

She did believe him. It scared her he was so persistent.

She said boldly, 'You know perfectly well, because I've told you before, that I don't want to go out with you, Mr Mitchell. Ever. So leave me alone or I'll report you for pestering me.'

He gave a mocking laugh.

'Who is going to report who, I'd like to know?'

She gave a shudder as he grasped her wrist.

The question came into her head. How long could she put up with this awful man bullying her? How long could she go on living on tenterhooks? Trying to protect Annette and herself she'd been drawn into this dreadful situation.

Just as she stood longing for some inspiration to deal with the situation to occur to her that would enable her to get rid of Gerry, she heard someone calling her.

'Nurse Cook!'

She jumped as she swung around to see Matron striding towards her, her flat shoes crunching on the gravel. Bristling with self-importance, and crackling in her starched uniform, with a disapproving look on her face, she frightened, not only Katherine, but Gerry, too, who slid away like the snake he was.

Never had Katherine been so pleased to see Matron, who was well known for appearing at any time.

'What did that man want?' Matron asked, coming up to Katherine.

Hearing Gerry's car start and out of the corner of her eye seeing it move off, Katherine gulped.

'He was a patient who came in for an appendix . . .'

'Appendectomy?'

'Yes, Matron.'

'What's his name?'

'Gerry Mitchell, Matron.'

'Ah, yes, Mr Mitchell,' Matron said, as if she remembered something about him, and it made Katherine look up into her startling cornflower blue eyes she'd never noticed before behind her glasses. How could a strict matron have such kindly blue eyes? Perhaps she wasn't quite the ogre all the young nurses thought she was. And when Matron asked, 'Has he been bothering you?' Katherine was disarmed.

'Yes, Matron. He has. He asked me

out and I said I didn't want to go. I've been on night duty and I hoped he'd forgotten about me. Then . . . ' she found herself give a shiver and looked down at the ground in embarrassment as tears appeared in her eyes. 'Well, you saw he came in his new car and wanted to take me for a ride.'

It amazed Katherine when Matron said in a soft voice, 'It isn't unusual for patients to have a crush on a nurse, you know. Just as a nurse may take a liking to one of the male medical staff.'

As Katherine had on Jack the porter.

'How can I get rid of Mr Mitchell, Matron?'

'I can report him to the police.'

'Oh, please don't do that!'

Matron looked at her young nurse sceptically.

'I mean,' Katherine said, 'I'm sure he will get the message that I really don't like him, and eventually he'll stop pestering me.'

'I wouldn't be too sure about that, Nurse Cook. Let me know if he continues to worry you.'

Katherine looked away and sighed. She still had another year at the hospital, even if she passed her second year exams. That was a long time for her to be worrying about avoiding Gerry Mitchell.

Matron asked, 'Is he the patient you thought had started the fire?'

Could she lie to Matron again? Then Katherine recalled that Martin had said that one of the patients could have started the fire, and it may not have been Annette.

'Yes, Matron,' she said, nodding, 'I think Mr Mitchell could well have started the fire.'

'I thought so. Another patient told me she'd seen him smoking, so I wondered about him . . . '

Katherine had the awful feeling Matron could see into her very soul, and she stood before the senior nurse wondering what would happen next.

What she didn't expect was that another smart car would drive up outside the Nurses' Home, and Martin Holt would get out of it.

'Why, hello,' Martin said breezily as his well-suited figure came towards them. 'Bullseye! Two ladies I'm pleased to see.'

Katherine was amazed when Matron shook hands with Mr Martin Holt, greeting him like an old friend instead of Jack the porter. But then, on reflection, Katherine realised that Matron would know Jack's true identity.

But Katherine was even more amazed — and embarrassed — when Martin faced her and kissed her on the cheek. Making her turn as brightly coloured as her hair.

'So this is the nurse you have your eye on, Mr Holt,' Matron said, smiling. 'I'll leave you and get on with my business.'

And she immediately bustled away into the Nurses' Home.

Katherine was hardly aware that Matron had gone as she looked up into the familiar face she'd missed seeing.

She didn't know whether to be happy to see him, or to be angry he'd abandoned her and had now turned up as if he hadn't forgotten her for weeks on end!

Martin sensed she was annoyed.

'I missed you, but because you've been on night duty you probably haven't had the time to get in touch with me — '

'I did phone you!' Katherine retorted, almost in tears again with happiness to see him, yet still furious with him for presuming she hadn't tried to contact him.

'You did?'

'I rang your mother. Twice.'

He looked puzzled, concerned.

'I'm not living at home now. I've moved.'

'Your mother didn't tell me where you'd gone. She said you'd been away for the weekend. And when I asked her where you were, she said to ring your office.' Katherine's voice rose in indignation. 'And how was I supposed to know where that was?'

He looked incredulous as he studied her cross face.

'Katherine,' he said, studying her face, 'I apologise, for myself and for my mother. I shouldn't have been so wrapped up in moving that I forgot to tell you my new address and telephone number. And my mother has been — '

'Rude!'

'I'm sure she didn't mean to be.'

'I'm sure she doesn't like me.'

Aware that a group of nurses had just trooped down the steps of the Nurses' Home and were staring in surprise at Nurse Cook and Jack having an argument, Katherine blushed.

Martin said, 'Come out to my car and we'll have a chat there. Better still, why don't I take you out to a hotel I know that serves great grub? I'll get you back in time for you to change into your uniform and go on duty.'

Did she really want to continue her relationship with Martin, knowing he put her far down the list of things that were important to him, like supporting his mother and excusing her abruptness? And thinking of moving house without letting her know where he'd gone? He hadn't once picked up the phone during the last two months to ask if things were all right, knowing Gerry Mitchell was after her.

She hesitated. Was it time to say goodbye to Martin?

But a little voice inside her told her that she should at least hear his excuses. Being attracted to him meant she couldn't just throw his friendship away.

Anyway, she knew she was tired after her spell on night duty. She badly needed a break.

Worried about the confrontation she'd just had with Gerry Mitchell, it might be a good idea to let him take her out so he could explain his behaviour, and heal the rift between them.

She hadn't any other person on this earth who knew the fix she was in, and Martin had offered to help her — even if he'd let her down.

'Yes, I'll go,' she said. She thought he

smiled with relief. 'But I'm not dressed up to go out.' Her twin-set was well worn, and her skirt, too. But she'd some nice shoes on — not that he'd notice!

'Katherine you look fine,' he declared, looking her up and down, 'I particularly like your shoes.'

Katherine liked her second-hand court shoes in cream leather, too, and felt pleased he'd noticed them.

It would be entirely different getting into Martin's car, as opposed to Gerry's car, and driving out into the countryside for a nice meal in a nearby small town. There was no doubt in her mind at all that, despite the misunderstanding his mother had caused, she trusted him enough to go out with him.

'It would be lovely to get away for a few hours,' she said dreamily, looking away from the hospital buildings. Days out, away from hospital work, were rare — especially for student nurses. And being with Martin with his gentlemanly ways would be an extra thrill.

Even if she would never get on with his mother, she thought at least they could be friends. Go out together occasionally, which would be fun.

But her spirits fell suddenly after he asked, 'Have you heard from Gerry Mitchell?'

Being thrown back into her worries about Gerry, Katherine replied, 'Yes, the wretched man came to see me just before you turned up. He was as cocky as ever. Matron shooed him away.'

'Most bullies are cowards,' he remarked, taking her elbow gently but firmly in a manner she found reassuring — so unlike the way Gerry had grasped her — and he escorted her to his car.

He opened the car door for her and, sliding in, she felt thrilled to be treated like a princess. He may not be the bodyguard she needed, but he made a superb ladies' man. And she looked forward to their day out.

His car smelt gloriously of new leather, and he drove with great care and attention, even though his car could get up to a fast speed easily if he'd wanted it to. But Martin, she knew, would always be a careful driver.

The sun came out as they drove sedately out of the Stamford. And Katherine relaxed and smiled, feeling like a contented cat enjoying the warmth of the sunshine.

So In Love

It was so sunny in the car that they had to put the car blinds down to protect their eyes from the strong sunlight. The green fields and huge oak trees, the quietly grazing cows and sheep they passed, were soothing to Katherine's mind.

She reasoned she really couldn't blame Martin for the difficulty she was in. She'd decided to protect Annette, to lie to Matron, and consequently she had Gerry breathing down her neck, threatening he would expose her secret if she didn't do as he wanted.

So she must accept the consequences of her decision. No-one else was in her shoes. It was her guilt and her misery. Not Martin's. She must just be grateful that he'd listened to her tale of woe and had offered to assist her.

Arriving at the town Katherine soon

saw the painted sign, *The Talbot*. As they were early for lunch, the car park was almost empty as they drove into it.

'It's a pretty place,' Katherine remarked, looking back down the street when they got out of the car.

'Shall we have a look around before we eat?' Martin suggested. 'The weather is perfect and there aren't many people here so we shouldn't find it difficult to get a table in half-an-hour.'

'Ooh, yes.' Katherine was delighted to be able to explore.

They were able to stretch their legs walking around the town's stone buildings, which had the look of ancient times.

Martin said, 'There are several very old inns here. You can see where coaches entered the yards and the travellers got out to refresh themselves after being bumped about for hours.'

Katherine was so intrigued. Looking through the archways made her feel as if she was living back in those coaching inn days.

'The inhabitants obviously feel proud of their houses,' she remarked, looking at the hanging baskets brimming with colourful cascading geraniums, busy lizzy, and lobelia plants.

'I thought you'd like it here,' Martin said, taking her hand and giving it a gentle squeeze.

It was indeed a magical time for Katherine, strolling down the street, holding hands with the man she now realised she loved, despite everything. She couldn't blame him for his mother's sharp tongue. His strong, warm hand made her feel wanted. Protected.

But did he feel the same about her?

They visited the elegant old church, with its tall spire and, stepping into the cool interior, they experienced its peacefulness. Katherine prayed that the burden of Gerry Mitchell's behaviour would soon leave her.

Walking in unison back to the pub she said, 'I've enjoyed looking around this town. Do you often go out to see new areas?'

'I do. Although, like you, my free time is limited.'

'What do you like to do when you're not working?'

'Lots of things.'

That sounded as though he did many exciting things. She had a lot to learn about him.

'What for example?' she asked.

'I play rugby.'

'That's a rough sport.'

He grinned.

'You get used to seeing a little blood. You must come and see a game some time and meet the lads.'

Katherine smiled back at him. It sounded like something to look forward to. That was, of course, if he didn't forget he'd asked her.

They walked to the river and then turned back towards the town.

The blackboard at the hotel had a chalk-written list of ordinary fare. It was a treat for Katherine to have the choice of food instead of her usual hospital meals.

She couldn't decide what she wanted. It all looked good to her, so she kept re-reading the list on the board.

'I'm going for sausage, mash and onion gravy,' Martin said. 'What would you like, Katherine?'

'Oh dear, I can't decide.'

'Try the special. The chicken pie is good here, my mother tells me.'

Katherine gulped.

'I'll have the fish pie, please.'

When they'd ordered what they wanted they went to a table by the casement window, which looked out over the garden, with their drinks.

'Do you come here a lot?' she asked.

'Occasionally. Mother loves this place,' he replied.

She bristled. Why had he spoilt her enjoyable day out by continually mentioning his mother?

He didn't seem to notice the hostility he'd aroused in her.

After a few minutes silence he asked, 'Are you all right, Katherine? Not sitting in a draught?'

'I'm not your mother,' she snapped back. 'I don't feel draughts.'

He chuckled.

'No, no, you're warm-blooded.'

Not sure if that was supposed to be a compliment, she asked, 'Are you, too?'

'Definitely.'

'So you've had other girlfriends?'

'A few but — '

'Your mother doesn't like them?'

He laughed.

'Oh, she likes Jilly Masters. Jilly, she thinks, is just right for me.'

Katherine blinked at him.

'But I don't.' His fist closed around his glass and he picked it up to take a sip of the liquid.

'You don't like Jilly, then?'

Martin smiled.

'I had enough of Jilly during the weekend they came to stay with us.'

Katherine's finger played with her beer mat.

'Your mother told me you went away for the weekend.'

'No.' He shook his head. 'We didn't go away.'

His mother had lied to her!

Martin continued, 'They came to stay with us. And we went out together, Mum, and her friend, Joan, and her daughter, Jilly, and me. We went to the theatre one evening, The Playhouse in Peterborough — to see a comedy, which the ladies enjoyed. And on Sunday we went to the Botanical Gardens at Kew.'

'Very nice,' Katherine remarked dryly.

'Oh, don't misunderstand me, Katherine. They are pleasant people, Jilly, and her mother. I've known them all my life because Jilly's mother was my mother's old school friend.'

'I see.'

He leant forward and, looking straight into her eyes, he said, 'It isn't as good as being out with you, Katherine.'

The waitress was bringing their meal on a tray. And despite Katherine's curiosity to know more about Jilly, the tempting food made her forget her, and she was able to tuck into her delicious fish meal. And Martin seemed to enjoy his, wolfing it down.

When they had finished they sat back and enjoyed a cup of coffee. Talking about the hospital staff, and then about his new accommodation, which was in one of the old houses in Stamford.

'Of course, I won't be staying with Tom for long. I'm looking around for a place of my own.'

'Won't Mother mind?'

His cup clattered down into the saucer.

'Whether she approves or not, I intend to find a place of my own. You see, I was only staying with my mother to be with her after my father died to keep her company until she found her feet. But that was several months ago. I always intended to find a home of my own. Only now I don't know what house I want — there are so many beautiful houses in and around Stamford.'

'You're lucky to be able to buy a house.'

'Yes, I am. But I have a problem.'

'Oh, yes?'

'Yes,' he said. 'I don't know yet what my future will be . . . I'm wondering . . . '

He was looking at her as if she had the answer to his problem — whatever that was.

Well, don't look at me for the answer, Katherine thought. Ask your mother.

She looked at her watch.

'I must get back. Or I'll be late on duty. Although Matron knows we are going out together, I doubt if that will be a good enough excuse if I'm late.'

He finished his coffee in one gulp and they got up to go.

'Matron's not unreasonable,' he said, 'She was most understanding when I offered to do the porter's job, and she allowed me to remain anonymous, with the name Jack.'

Katherine nodded. She had discovered Matron had a soft side, too.

Walking out of the pub Martin brought up the subject of his mother again.

'My mother said she would like to meet you,' he said suddenly, as if he'd been thinking about it.

Katherine didn't want to say exactly what she thought about that idea!

She had no intention of being hauled up in front of his over-protective mother whose son was still tied to her apron strings.

'Well, I'm very busy taking exams at present,' she said dismissively.

'Well, I understand your exams must come first. But Mother is keen to meet you.'

What could she say? Nothing polite came into her mind which could excuse her from having to meet his mother.

And she had the problem of avoiding Gerry Mitchell.

As if reading her thoughts, he said, 'I must discuss Mr Mitchell with you on the way home.'

She thought it was preferable to talking about his mother.

Opening the car door for her, Martin said, 'I told you in my letter that I had been making enquires about Gerry Mitchell. But I haven't got very far because I've been moving and playing a lot of rugby.'

'Oh, have you?' she muttered, slipping in the car. She knew now what his priorities were, and they were certainly not her and her troubles.

He went around to the other side of the car and slid into the driver's seat, starting the engine and driving the car out into the road.

'Martin,' she said, 'there's a chemist over there. And a newsagent. Can you stop for a few moments while I pop in and do some shopping? I was going out this morning when Gerry stopped me, and I really do need a few things. I'll be quick.'

'Of course,' he said, slowing the car and parking it near the shop.

She left him sitting in his car as she hurried in to get the few items she wanted, thinking he was the kind of man who was easy to ask to do things for her. He was indeed kind and comfortable to be with.

She wondered if Jilly loved him? As much as she did?

When she returned, he started the car engine saying, 'Don't get me wrong about Gerry Mitchell. As an accountant, I frequently have to probe into clients financial affairs like a detective. I have to find out how it is that Mr Mitchell, who works as a baker, can afford a luxury lifestyle.

'I'm aware he's a thoroughly slippery character and you must keep well away from him. As you were on night duty, I knew you were safe. But the moment you came off night duty, the wretched man turned up — and that worries me.'

'Not half as much as it worries me!'

When he proceeded to tell her that he had found out that Gerry worked at a local bakery, and to give her advice about how to avoid him, Katherine only half listened, because she knew she had to rely on her own judgement in the end. Martin had let her down once — or his mother had prevented him from helping her.

Regretfully Katherine knew she couldn't count on him to be there to help her when she really needed him.

'Thank you for a lovely day out,' Katherine said as he pulled up outside the Nurses' Home.

'It's been a pleasure. And I look forward to having many more outings with you, Katherine. I'll be in touch, but be sure to ring me if you need help. Here's my telephone number.' He scribbled down his new telephone number and Katherine was glad she wouldn't have to get past his mother to get to speak to him.

A couple of nurses walking by spotted them and turned to each other to smile and whisper.

Katherine said to Martin, as she stepped out of the car, and they walked together up to the front door of the Nurses' Home, 'It will be all over the hospital now that you are taking me out.'

He smiled at her.

'I'm not working here any longer and I'm very proud to be your boyfriend,' he said, stooping to give her a kiss.

She gave him a wide smile back.

'I'm pleased, too,' she said. Although she thought she would be even more pleased if Jilly Masters and Gerry Mitchell — and his mother — were not spoiling their romance.

A Strange Encounter

Arriving back at the hospital, Katherine had to say goodbye to Martin quickly as she had to race up to her room and get changed into her uniform.

She was soon back on the wards and immersed in her nursing work. And in the evenings, she had so much studying to do for her examinations, she largely forgot about Martin — and Gerry.

Several days later, when Annette and Katherine became fed up with revision, and because their first examination was next day, they sneaked into the empty Staff Nurses' Lounge to watch television.

Having a laugh at the cartoon on the box, they suddenly froze when they heard some nurses coming into the lobby. Were they senior nurses who would give them a good telling off for going into their lounge?

Katherine quickly turned the television off. She and Annette guiltily tiptoed out of the room. But they only got as far as the nurses' pantry and hid in there as the staff nurses came by.

'I'm sure it was him,' one of the nurses said, flopping down on a sofa.

The other replied, 'Well, I haven't seen him on duty for months. Maybe he's got himself another job?'

'I saw these two smart-suited men coming towards me in town, they were chatting so they didn't notice me. I was so surprised to see Jack that I didn't say, hello, because I couldn't understand why he was so well dressed.'

'If we were allowed to go out in our nurses' uniform, I dare say he might have recognised me, because he was always pleasant to everyone, was Jack.'

'Seems as if he'd made it from rags to riches in one easy move. Can you tell me how he did it?'

'Maybe he won the football pools.'

The girls laughed.

The other girl sat down on an easy

chair and kicked off her shoes. Wriggling her toes, she said, 'I heard one of the second year student nurses was going out with Jack.'

'Ooh! Lucky thing. Who?'

'Katherine Cook.'

'Well, she sure gets around. I heard she was going out with an ex-patient who is often hanging around outside the Nurses' Home.'

Katherine heard no more because Annette quietly closed the door.

Returning to the student lounge, Annette asked, 'Are you going out with Jack?'

'Can you keep a secret?'

Annette nodded.

'I have been out with him.'

'That's wonderful!' Annette exclaimed. 'I'm so happy for you. Is it true he has left the hospital?'

Katherine nodded.

'Yes, he was only here temporarily.' She went on to explain the reason for him working at the hospital, and added, 'Don't tell everyone, will you? I don't know if he wants it spread around.'

'I can't think why not. If he worked here to replace the porter he accidentally injured it shows he has a superb sense of justice. It can't have been easy for him to take the hospital job. I admire him for doing it.'

'He told me many people do voluntary work.'

Annette thought a moment and said, 'Yes, I suppose some people do. But I still admire him for it.'

'So do I. But as far as anything romantic is concerned, he's a dead loss. He's a mummy's boy.'

Annette looked surprised.

'I wouldn't have thought he was. He always struck me as a man quite capable of looking after his own affairs. And a kind man, too.'

Without having to explain to Annette why she thought Martin wasn't a man she would consider marrying, Katherine said, 'Well, he is.' Reluctant to say anything more about him — even to explain his name was Martin, not Jack

— because thinking about him brought on pangs of longing to see him again.

She said, 'I'm off to bed now. See you in the morning. And don't you worry about your exams. You'll do well.'

Annette seemed disappointed she was not going to be told more about Jack.

Katherine, however, didn't want to discuss Martin even with her best friend.

Annette said, 'I'm going to collect some of my books I left in the lounge, then I'm going to my room, too.'

Going upstairs to her bedroom, Katherine felt disturbed that the nurses had been discussing her going out with Martin. Nurses could be so inquisitive. They diagnosed each others' love lives like they did illnesses. And Katherine couldn't allow anyone to find out about the real trouble she was in.

She felt almost thankful she had some exams to take. It took her mind off her other difficulties.

* * *

Weeks later the examinations were, like most exams, taken, talked about, and stewed over for a while, and then they were forgotten — until the results came out.

Katherine felt she couldn't be cooped up in the hospital for too long without turning into a hospital bug.

She decided she must go out. She needed to take a break from the antiseptic smell, and the constant bed-making.

She thought, as the auction rooms were not far away, she could slip out and see if there were any second-hand shoes in the sale. There was a preview that day and there would be many people there.

It was enjoyable for Katherine to wander about seeing what she could find of interest at the auction.

After looking around the saleroom she found nothing that would interest her, but to her amusement there was

111

one lot she looked at, fascinated.

A pair of miniature shoes.

Delightful. Small and exquisitely made. Cream floral shoes — but surely well out of her price range.

Katherine thought it was a sensible idea to collect miniature shoes. They took up less room and could be displayed in a room cabinet.

'Aren't they pretty?' A voice beside her made Katherine turn her head to see a well-dressed, middle-aged lady standing by her. The lady's lined but attractive face was lit up as she picked up one of the shoes to examine it closely.

'I expect you have your eye on them,' the lady said, 'and as you saw them first I won't outbid you if you want them.' She put them carefully back on the display table.

Katherine thought how kind of the lady to say that, but assured her, 'Oh, I can't have them.'

The lady smiled at her as if to enquire, why not?

Katherine felt she had to explain. 'My mother says I have too many shoes already.'

The lady gave a tinkled laugh. 'She is probably right, my dear. But shoe collectors can never have enough.'

Katherine liked her. She chuckled as she said, 'That's true. But I collect real shoes, not miniature ones. And Mum can hardly walk in my room for shoes at home.'

'Maybe you should start a miniature shoe collection. They take up far less room.'

Katherine thought about it.

'Mmm. Maybe I should.'

The lady looked down at the shoes Katherine was wearing. 'The shoes you are wearing are beautifully made.'

Katherine glanced at her shoes.

'They are. They are second-hand, of course. Pre-war and a little big for me, but I stuff a little paper in the toes because I love to wear them.'

Katherine wondered why she was talking so freely to a stranger. But shoes were their topic of conversation, and when the lady suggested they both went for a cup of coffee at one of the most expensive coffee shops in Stamford, Katherine regretted she had to say no, she couldn't afford it.

The lady, however, seemed determined she should go with her, saying, 'The coffee will be on me, my dear. It'll be nice to chat to you about our love of shoes.'

It was a treat too good to be missed, and Katherine immediately said yes, she'd like to go.

It struck Katherine that the lady might live alone and be a little lonely. And being a nurse, she was well aware of the need to provide a little cheerful companionship to people. It was just as necessary as medicine.

But it certainly wasn't an effort to talk to the lady. They got on like a house on fire.

How long they sat there exchanging information on their shoe collections, Katherine didn't know. They enjoyed two cups of coffee and a cream cake!

'I must go now,' Katherine said, looking hurriedly at her watch. 'I'm on duty in fifteen minutes.'

'Yes, you'd better, my dear.'

'Thanks for the coffee.'

'Not at all. It was a great pleasure chatting with you, Miss . . . ?'

'Cook. Katherine Cook.'

Just as Katherine walked out of the coffee shop the lady called after her, 'Where do you work?'

'I'm a probationer nurse at the hospital.'

Katherine was puzzled to see the lady's face look a little stricken. Had she said something wrong?

She couldn't imagine why, but she had to hurry away in case she was late on duty.

* * *

Katherine's mother had rung her, she learned, as she entered the Nurses' Home.

Knowing it was about time she visited her mum, she felt guilty about enjoying coffee and creams cakes in a posh coffee house when she should have got on her bike to see her mother.

Next time I'm off duty I will see Mum, she vowed.

So the next time she finished her shift, when she went to sign out, she was amazed to find a small parcel waiting for her.

She picked it up, turning it over and over in her hands. It had been hand delivered. Opening it, she was amazed to see the miniature shoes she'd seen for sale at the auction.

'How kind. How very kind of her,' she murmured as she picked up the note inside the parcel and read, *For Katherine. With thanks for a wonderful morning discussing old boots to high heels*.

Katherine knew what it meant and smiled.

She was disappointed, however, that the lady hadn't left a message or even her name so that Katherine could thank her.

She looked at the pretty miniature shoes and kissed them.

'I'll always treasure you,' she said, slipping back to her room to put them on her bookshelf. She hoped that one day she might bump into that kind lady shoe collector again at a sale.

★ ★ ★

Maybe it was because Katherine was overjoyed to have the little shoes given to her, or because her mind was in the clouds, she wasn't concentrating enough on the traffic.

Huge lorries thundered by her, making her bike wobble. And when a stray dog decided to cross the road in front of her, she braked to avoid it, but the brakes' squeals frightened the little beast, which ran across the road and it was hit by a passing car.

Appalled, Katherine immediately

propped her bike up against a wall and, being a nurse, Katherine's instinct was to assist the howling, injured animal. She gently picked it up and carried it off the busy road.

The traffic continued to whiz by, as if the accident hadn't happened.

She could tell the poor mite needed medical care. She frowned, wondering where the nearest veterinary surgery was, and remembered seeing one in the main street. She put the little animal in her bicycle basket and wheeled it there.

It took some time to see the vet and to have the poor little dog examined. When the vet said, 'His hind leg is broken, I'll need to set it,' Katherine became the sensible nurse she was and stayed to comfort the little creature until the vet could put it to sleep to have the operation.

But of course she worried about who would pay the vet's bill.

Who would be kind enough to lend her the money?

Only one name came to mind: Martin Holt.

The vet was happy for her to use his phone.

She rang Martin's office and was relieved to hear his voice.

'Hello, Martin Holt here.'

'Martin, it's Katherine.'

'Are you in trouble?'

'Yes, I mean not me. I need ask you a favour.' She felt hot with embarrassment.

'Ask away.'

'When I was going to see my mum this morning, I saw a dog get run over — I mean it was injured — '

'Was it killed?'

'No. But I took it to the vet and I . . . ' to Katherine's horror she began to sob.

It was not as if she wasn't used to seeing people in pain, but the small helpless animal was so vulnerable. For some reason she felt a bit like that herself.

'Katherine, where are you?'

She sniffed.

'At the vet.'

'In the High Street?'

It took Katherine a few seconds to control her tears to mumble, 'Yes.'

He recognised at once that she was in tears and he said, 'Stay there. I'm coming over right away,' before he put down the receiver.

Fortunately, the vet had a box of tissues to hand her.

'I'm sorry to be making a fuss,' Katherine said, still crying.

The vet looked at her sympathetically.

'It's always emotional for an owner when their pet is injured.'

Katherine explained it wasn't her dog. Because having rescued it and comforted it, she'd become like a caring owner. Watching its furry face asleep in the recovery cage, she wanted to protect it.

And part of her knew she was crying because of all the distress she'd suffered recently, with Gerry Mitchell baiting her, her examinations, and now because of the accident, she would be late getting to her mum's who'd be expecting her — and she couldn't pay the vet bill!

A Hardened Nurse

Katherine was sitting in the vet's waiting-room feeling a right fool. She still had the box of tissues on her lap. The veterinary nurse kept looking at her uncertainly, and she tried to give her a smile to reassure her that she wasn't going to break down again. Other pet owners were there, too, holding cages containing animals ranging from cats to hamsters, and a dog with a bandaged paw who looked pathetic with its head in a big plastic collar.

She closed her eyes so that people might think she wasn't well and not just a cry baby.

'Ben Buckly,' the vet called, and the man with the limping dog got on his feet and led the animal into the vet's consulting room.

'Katherine.' She opened her eyes again to find Martin Holt standing in front of her. There was a questioning expression on his face as he sat down beside her and removing the box of tissues he clasped her hands. 'Are you OK?'

'Yes,' she whispered, aware that several pairs of ears were able to listen to what she said, 'I just felt upset about the dog.'

She had objected before when she had felt he'd treated her like his mother, but now his thoughtfulness was most welcome. She was thankful he was the kind and caring man she knew he was.

He said nothing more, but sat close to her.

'I feel a right twit,' she managed to say at last, dabbing her eyes. 'Anyone would think I was a fainting first year nurse seeing her first operation. Not a hardened nurse.'

Martin gave her a rueful smile.

'My dear girl,' he said softly, 'there's

nothing hard about you. You wouldn't be here now — and with your other worries — if you were.'

She looked sideways up at him saying, 'Then I'm an impulsive, stubborn woman, who asks for trouble. If I had any sense, I wouldn't be in my shoes.'

He gave a chuckle and taking her hand gave it a comforting squeeze.

'I'm glad you are the way you are,' he whispered in her ear.

Then they both sat in silence. It wasn't necessary to say anything, because they recognised they were right about themselves — and each other.

They knew they were a soft-hearted couple.

She moved closer to him and whispered, 'I'm afraid I can't afford to pay the vet bill.'

His hand felt inside his jacket and he drew out his cheque book.

'I think I can manage that,' he said. 'The real problem is going to be, what are you going to do with the injured dog?'

Katherine hadn't thought of that.

He gave her hand another gentle squeeze, then he got up and walked to the receptionist's desk. After asking the receptionist a few questions, Katherine saw him write a cheque.

Returning to her a little while later, he said, 'Well, that's that done.'

Katherine's eyes looked up at him.

'What will happen to the dog?'

'Come along. That's settled, too.'

Mystified, Katherine took the hand he offered her and stood up. As they walked out of the veterinary's waiting-room he explained.

'I'll tell you what's going to happen to it. My mother is going to have it. She likes looking after things, especially now she's lost me. She needs a new pet! And she likes animals — especially dogs. She has a large garden, which is well fenced in. And she lives in a village and will be delighted to take it for walks.'

'What if your mother doesn't get on with it?'

'I'm sure she will look after it until it is well again.'

'What if the dog is claimed by its owner?'

'Oh, my mother is a sensible lady and will understand if that happens. But I understand from the veterinary nurse that the vet had written on his report that the poor animal has been badly treated, so the true owner is unlikely to come forward. Your little dog will get a fine new home.'

Katherine wasn't so sure it would, living with his mother. But she thanked him.

'I can pay for the dog's licence,' she offered.

He laughed.

'No need. My mother will sort that out.'

Martin had a way of sorting things out, too, Katherine thought. They were out in the street, but she stood on tiptoe and kissed his cheek.

Drops of water fell on them. It was starting to rain heavily.

'Oh dear!' Katherine cried. 'Now I'm going to get soaked. I haven't a raincoat or umbrella.'

'The house I'm staying in is just up the street, so why don't we go there to shelter for a while?'

Katherine looked up at the steel grey sky and shuddered.

'I have my bike here.'

'Leave it. I can run you back to the hospital by car and I'll collect your bicycle later.'

* * *

Dashing along the wet pavement with their collars up and heads down, they arrived panting at a Georgian house's front door, which Martin opened and they both tumbled in.

They were soaked to the skin and shivering.

Katherine stood looking at the gracious interior while she dripped on to the tiled floor. She began making puddles on the tiles where she stood.

127

'You'd better get those wet things off,' Martin remarked, taking off his jacket and shaking it like a dog, splattering water everywhere.

She shivered again, putting her hand through her soaked hair.

'I think you need a hot bath and some dry clothes,' Martin told her. 'Although you'll have to wear something of mine until I get yours washed and dried.

'Ah, my cleaning lady is here. She'll see to it. Mrs Buxton, can you run Katherine a bath and see to her clothes?'

'Of course, Mr Holt,' she replied.

He dived upstairs, taking the steps two at a time and calling back to her, 'I'll just get you something to wear.'

It did seem a little too personal to be having a bath in a stranger's home, but with Mrs Buxton overseeing them, she had no time to object.

Any other man, she thought, might make her feel embarrassed, but somehow she accepted that Martin was not intending to do anything other than to make her comfortable.

On going upstairs she found the bathroom was becoming warm with the steam from the hot water. On the towel rail was a fluffy bath towel, and what looked like his bathrobe was hanging on the door hook.

'Mrs B's put out some hair shampoo, but I'm afraid I haven't any nice bath salts for you,' he said. 'I know my mother likes some. So you'll just have to pretend I've put some in.'

Mrs Buxton stood outside the door while she took off her wet outer clothes and handed them to her.

It was heavenly to soak in the warming water.

But she couldn't stay there for long, because Martin needed to warm himself in the hot tub, too. Reluctantly she got out and dried herself as fast as she could.

Putting on the bathrobe, and some extremely large mules he'd left for her, she opened the bathroom door a crack and peered out of the bathroom to see him waiting on the landing.

She had no time to feel embarrassed, because he came and strode past her into the bathroom saying, 'There's a fire downstairs in the kitchen range. And there's a fresh pot of tea and some of Mrs Buxton's scones.'

The bathroom door slammed and she heard the taps running fast and he began to sing. Katherine was amused to hear the words of a bawdy rugby song as she went downstairs.

Remembering it was not Martin's house — it belonged to his friend, Tom, she couldn't learn much about him from the belongings she saw lying about.

She was glad it wasn't his mother's house. If it were, she'd be afraid to touch anything.

News Of Gerry Mitchell

Katherine found the old-fashioned kitchen with its tiled floor and scrubbed wooden kitchen table and plate rack. The teapot and teacups were sitting out. A china plate of delicious looking scones was also on the table.

Her clothes had been draped on the clothes horse, but she feared they would take for ever to dry. Even her shoes had been loosely stuffed with crumpled newspaper and left by the range.

She was experiencing how nice it was to be nursed, instead of having all the nursing to do herself.

She glanced at the kitchen clock and suddenly thought about her mum, who was expecting her.

When she heard Martin coming towards the kitchen she started to pour the tea.

'Hello. Had a nice bath?' she asked in her nurse's voice.

He was fully dressed, and smiled at her.

'Yes, thank you. And I trust you are feeling OK now. I must say you look adorable in my bathrobe.'

Going pink, she ignored his remark.

'I'm afraid I have another difficulty now.'

He looked at her enquiringly as she seemed to be unable to tell him. This was because she felt a strong desire to go up to him and plant a kiss on his cheek. Indeed it would be very nice if he kissed her.

'Go on,' he said with the understanding voice of a sympathetic doctor. 'What is it?'

She gulped.

'I was going to see my mother when the dog was hit.'

'You mean, she will be worried you haven't come?'

Katherine poured the tea into the cups and said, 'Yes. And my clothes are still too wet to put on.'

'Don't worry about that. We'll soon sort that out.'

He didn't tell her to give her mother a ring. He went to a cupboard and took out a packet of biscuits which he opened.

'As it's still raining, I'll go around in my car to see her if you wish. And get you some dry clothes. But we should have tea first.'

They sat at the scrubbed wooden kitchen table opposite each other.

He didn't look like a softie. His wide shoulders and athletic build showed he was a sportsman.

'What sports do you play?' she asked him.

That set him off. Talking about his love of rugby, swimming and tramping around the countryside. She could easily imagine him doing all of that.

'How about you? What do you do in your free time?'

'Oh, I like playing tennis. They have just made a tennis court for the nurses at the hospital, but I'm not much good at it. I like to swim, too — and take a country walk when I get the opportunity.'

'Perhaps we could go for walks in the country? Get some fresh air if we can avoid the fertiliser spread on the fields!'

'I'd like that. It'll make a change to get away from the hospital smells!'

They laughed.

Katherine now felt she could tell him anything, so she added, 'I also collect second-hand shoes.'

'I noticed you wear quality shoes.'

She was about to tell him that she went to auctions when the telephone's ring interrupted him.

'Excuse me,' he said, getting up. 'It's probably my office.'

She cleared away the tea things while he went into the hall to take the call. He was gone for some time.

He came back into the kitchen and kicked the door shut behind him, saying, 'That was the police.'

She almost dropped the tea pot she was drying.

'They had some news about Gerry Mitchell.'

Katherine looked at him, wide-eyed. The horrid man's image came to mind, with his threats.

She wasn't surprised to learn he was known to the police. Nurses had to tend sick people no matter what kind of person they were — and she had. But being attacked by them was something else.

'I told you I was making some enquires about him.'

'Yes, you did,' Katherine said.

He looked at his watch.

'I'll explain it all to you. He's a known thief and was thrown out of the army. You're also not the only girl he's pestered. He's well known for it. Now, I ought to pop around and see your mother first if I'm to collect some clothes for you and get you back to go on duty on time.'

Katherine could only agree. Having worked shifts at the hospital, both of them knew how important it was for the hospital staff not to be late on duty. So she withheld the questions she was longing to ask him and gave him her mother's address.

'Will you be all right for half-an-hour? Mrs Buxton had to go. The newspaper is in the hall if you want to see it. You can go into the sitting room if you like, but it's warmer in the kitchen. Any message for your mother?'

'Just tell her that I love her and apologise for me, will you? And I'll be over to see her as soon as I can.'

Martin Lets Katherine Down Again

It took Martin some time to reach Katherine's mother's house, because he was doing his best to concentrate on driving carefully in the heavy rain.

He was concerned about avoiding wobbly cyclists and splashing them, because huge puddles were forming at the side of road.

His mind was returning to think of Katherine constantly. Picturing her looking surprisingly elegant dressed in his bathrobe, with her small feet in his mules. Her shiny auburn hair she'd combed, and curls he did not normally see under her nurse's cap, resting delightfully over her shoulders.

But now he was going to see her mother. He'd been told she was a widow — her husband had died bravely during the war. He felt he had to intrude carefully into the close mother and daughter relationship without upsetting Mrs Cook. Having experience in dealing with his own mother, he hoped he would be successful.

After ringing the front door bell, he smiled at the small lady who opened the door. She looked very like an older version of Katherine.

'Good morning, Mrs Cook. I've come to bring a message from your daughter, Katherine.'

The sceptical look on Mrs Cook's face told him he'd already made a mistake.

She said rather huffily, 'My daughter, Kitty, isn't here.'

Martin could have kicked himself. He remembered Katherine telling him that a strange man had been waiting around her mother's house, and it had worried her. She might think he was that man. He coughed.

'I beg your pardon, Mrs Cook. Kitty calls herself Katherine at the hospital.'

Oh dear, she didn't like that, either. She began to close the door, muttering, 'I don't know who you're talking about young man.'

Before she'd actually shut the door, he said quickly, 'She was coming to see you on her bicycle this morning, but she's been waylaid and has asked me to tell you she is sorry she can't come to see you today.'

Mrs Cook's eyes peered around the door, which stood ajar. She looked him up and down.

'Who are you? A doctor from the hospital?'

'No, I'm a porter — or I was.'

That information didn't remove the look of suspicion from her face. And Martin began to think that, although Katherine had found his mother difficult, her mother wasn't going to be very easy to deal with, either.

'May I come in — it's raining out here.'

She looked unsure.

'I don't want you dripping all over

the hall carpet. Go round to the tradesman's entrance.'

With that less than courteous welcome, Martin grimaced as she shut the door in his face. He began to understand why Katherine had found his mother tricky to deal with. He went to the side gate feeling he was becoming just as drenched as he was before he'd had his bath.

Mrs Cook seemed in no hurry to open the back door, and Martin pulled his mac collar up as a trickle of rain rolled down his back. He thrust his hands into his pockets as another trickle of rain ran down his nose.

'Come in,' she said a little ungraciously, letting him into her kitchen.

Martin stood on the door mat dripping.

'I only came to say that Kath . . . Kitty, is sorry she can't come to see you this morning.'

She looked very like Katherine as she said, 'Oh. Why is that?'

He looked at the kitchen table. On it

was laid out the fruits of her labour: a sponge cake sprinkled with icing sugar, some home-made chocolate biscuits, and a plate of sandwiches.

Martin suddenly felt sorry for the lady. She'd been looking forward to seeing her daughter, and had made the effort to lay out a tasty spread for her — then a complete stranger had come to her door and told her she wasn't coming.

What could he say?

'Mrs Cook, I was wondering if I could take a slice of your delicious-looking cake to take back for Kitty? I know she would appreciate it. You do miss home comforts in the hospital, and she has been working very hard taking exams, as well as slaving away on the wards.'

Mrs Cook looked at him quizzically.

'Are her exams over?'

Martin didn't know how to reply to that.

'I think so,' he said lamely.

'So why can't she come and see me?

It's been ages since she came. Other nurses get time off . . . '

For a moment Martin felt like putting his arm around her shoulders as tears came into her eyes.

'She was coming, Mrs Cook, but she found an injured dog. She had to take it to a vet. So she hasn't time to come here today. But I'm sure she will come as soon as she gets more time off. Nurses in training get very little time off duty — I'm sure you know that.'

Mrs Cook looked at him more sympathetically.

He explained, 'She phoned me when she was at the vet's, asking me to . . . help her. It was raining hard and she can't bike here because she left her bike at the vet's. You see she got soaked . . . '

He wasn't telling it right. The last thing he wanted to say was that she'd gone back to his place for a bath!

'What's your name?' she asked abruptly.

'Martin Holt. But in the hospital I was known as Jack the porter.'

'Ah, yes, I do remember Kitty mentioning you.'

His eyes twinkled at her.

'My name is really Martin, but I was known as Jack at the hospital. Just as your Kitty calls herself Nurse Katherine Cook.'

'Does she now?'

'And your name is?'

Mrs Cook looked a little startled, but under Martin's friendly smile she replied, 'My name is Margaret.'

'There we are. All sorted out.'

'No, we're not. Why does everyone have to change their names? I think it's unnecessary.'

Like Katherine, her mother was stubborn.

'Well now, Margaret, Katherine told me she does not like being called Kitty — except by you, of course. Her real name, which is the name you gave her, is Katherine. She prefers it.'

'Yes, my husband liked the name Katherine. His father called her Kitty as a baby and the name stuck.'

Martin nodded.

'I'm sure she would be happy for you to continue calling her by the name you always have. But everyone else calls her Katherine, because she asked them to.'

Margaret sat down on one of the kitchen chairs.

'Why did you change your name?'

Martin gulped. Time was getting on and he had to get some clothes and take them back for Katherine. And now he would be delayed, explaining about his reason for working at the hospital. But he knew she had a right to know his private business — especially as he was courting her daughter.

'Have a cup of tea and a biscuit?' she said in a more friendly voice.

He felt it would be the wrong thing to rush away, Margaret wanted company for a while, so he stayed to talk to her.

* * *

Katherine in the meantime was feeling restless. She looked at the clock for the eightieth time. She only had twenty minutes to get back to the hospital and to go on duty.

Heaven knows what had happened to Martin.

The wretched man had let her down — again!

Finally, fed up with waiting, she let down the clothes horse and put on her damp skirt and blouse. Grabbing her shoes and handbag she left the house just as Martin's car came along the road.

Neither of them saw each other.

She almost ran to the vet's. Hoping the little dog was recovering, but not having enough time to enquire, she got on her bicycle and pedalled hard through the splashy puddles, getting sprayed by a few car wheels as she raced towards the Nurses' Home.

With her head down she didn't see the stationary bus parked at a bus stop and rode straight into the back of it!

Wham! Falling off her bike, Katherine cried out as the impact left her with a sore head, a bruised shoulder and injured arm. Also, she suffered a grazed knee — with a huge ladder in her stocking — and a bent front wheel!

Picking herself up as no-one was about to help her, she hobbled the rest of the way to the Nurses' Home, trying to manage her bike with a smashed wheel. She was tempted to leave her broken bike behind, but she had to get it mended, because she would need it again soon to visit her mum.

Rushing to change into her uniform was difficult, especially with her throbbing, sore arm, and she arrived at the women's surgical ward just as the ward sister remarked, 'I wonder what has happened to Nurse Cook? She isn't normally late.'

Looking up, she saw Katherine limping into the ward. A red graze down the side of her pale face looked sore, and she clutched her injured arm.

'Whatever's happened to you, Nurse Cook?'

'I rode into a bus.'

The ward sister didn't look very sympathetic.

'That was a silly thing to do! You'd better report to the nurses' doctor straight away. We have enough injuries in this ward without you adding to them.'

Katherine was almost crying as she turned to walk out of the ward. It wasn't her sore head, bruises and her painful, aching arm that had made her tearful. It was mainly because of that untrustworthy man, Martin Holt.

★ ★ ★

The nurses' doctor was sharp. It always surprised Katherine when she heard the charming bedside manner doctors used with their patients, that they were often less sympathetic treating the nurses. They were expected to stay healthy.

After examining her, Doctor Dean said, 'You look as if you've run into a bus.'

'Actually, I did,' Katherine said,

feeling stupid. 'I know it's big enough, but it was raining so hard and I was on my bike and pedalling with my head down and . . . ' she sneezed ' . . . so I just didn't see it.' She sneezed again. 'I crashed into it.'

On top of everything, was she getting a cold? It was difficult for her not to cry. But the doctor spotted she was upset and spoke in a more kindly manner.

'There, there, Nurse Cook. You need to lie down for a bit. But I want you to go for an x-ray first. I'm not happy about your right arm.'

Neither was Katherine. It ached terribly.

The doctor went to his desk and wrote on a pad, then after Katherine was dressed, he said, 'Give this to the sister at x-ray. When you have had your x-ray she will send the results to me. I won't put you in the staff ward — go to your bed in the Nurses' Home for a while. I'll ring Matron and she will get someone to look after you.'

'Thank you, Doctor,' Katherine said, sneezing again.

* ★ ★ ★

Martin was put out when he arrived at Tom's house, searched around and found Katherine wasn't there.

He looked at his watch and realised why she'd left — she'd wanted to get on duty on time. He was too late after finding it difficult to get away from her chatterbox mother.

Getting Mrs Cook to go upstairs and collect some dry clothes for Katherine seemed to take a lot of time while he waited patiently.

Margaret did eventually pack up a few items — but she'd become such a gossip, Martin had the greatest difficulty getting away from her. He did enjoy eating her sponge cake, though. His mother didn't make cakes.

'Your sponge cake is delicious,' he had said, picking up the last crumbs and putting them into his mouth.

Pleased, Margaret had chatted on about her love of cooking, and it being a waste of time without Kitty being there to enjoy it. She explained that her husband had died during the war. As, indeed, Martin's father had, so they were able to commiserate.

But time went on and Martin had known he must leave. The last thing he wanted was to sound as if he couldn't wait to leave the house.

He heaved a sigh of relief when he finally got away with a tin filled with a large piece of sponge cake wrapped in grease proof paper, and some of Margaret's home-made biscuits, as well as a change of clothes for Katherine.

Having found Katherine had left his friend's house, he drove to the hospital and asked at the reception desk if Nurse Cook had reported for duty.

'Why, Jack, you're looking smart today,' the receptionist said, smiling at the suited man. She was used to seeing him in his porter's uniform.

'Hi, Jack.' Another nurse passing by

recognised him, and he smiled back at her.

He didn't really like the attention he was getting, but he had to find out if Katherine was there.

After ringing the ward she was supposed to be on, the receptionist told him that Nurse Cook had had an accident and was being treated by a doctor.

'What? What's happened to her?' He felt shocked. 'Where is she?'

'I don't know, Jack.'

That put Martin's mind in a spin. Gerry Mitchell came to his mind. Had the wretched man been pestering her again?

He eventually found out, to his relief, that Katherine was safe and was tucked up in bed in the Nurses' Home.

Some Good News
From Matron

Katherine slept for a while, and then sat up in bed when her dinner was brought to her on a tray. Although her injuries were painful, she enjoyed the luxury of being a patient and being waited on for a change.

When there was a knock on the door, Katherine said, 'Come in,' expecting it to be Annette, or one of her friends. She gave a quiet gasp as Matron came in.

'How are you, Nurse Cook?'

Remembering Matron wasn't quite the terror the young nurses always thought she was, Katherine replied, 'I feel as if I've been through a mincer.'

Matron gave her a wry smile.

'Doctor Dean told me your arm has been broken and has been set.'

That explained the pain it was giving her. Katherine said, 'Oh dear. I won't be able to help much on the wards.'

'You won't be able to do anything, my dear. You'll have to go back home for a while and recover for a few weeks.'

Katherine's brain buzzed. 'But what about my training?'

Matron fingered her chin. 'Well, that is a problem of course. I would normally have to place you in the lower set —'

'A lower set?' Katherine was dismayed.

'But,' Matron looked into her horrified eyes and said, 'As you are a diligent nurse, and Sister Tutor tells me your knowledge of nursing is outstanding, and the staff nurses tell me your practical work is well up to standard . . .'

Katherine blushed. 'I'm not that good,' she muttered.

'Let me be the judge of that.'

'Yes, Matron.'

Matron's bosom heaved. 'So I have decided . . .'

Katherine held her breath.

'You are to go home for a while and take things easy. I will write to your mother and tell her what you can and can't do to help your arm heal.'

'Thank you, Matron.'

That was decided. There was nothing Katherine could do about it. It was a shame she would have to be put back in her studies.

Matron was looking out of the window and remarked, 'I'll have to tell the maid to remove the dust from your window sill.'

Katherine smiled. Matron was not at all keen on dust — or dirt of any kind. Her hospital had to be as clean as a scrubbed pan. Everywhere. Germs, that injured the sick, could thrive in dirty places and Matron would not give them houseroom.

'So now I'm going to tell you a secret,' Matron said suddenly and Katherine blinked.

'You have passed your exams with honours.'

Katherine almost whooped with joy and wanted to ask if Annette had too, but she dare not.

'So,' continued Matron, 'I can't see the point in holding you back. You will remain with your set and will be given some homework so you can continue your studies at home.'

Overjoyed, Katherine cried, 'Oh thank you, Matron. I will work hard on the wards as soon as I am better.'

Matron gave her one of her rare, lovely smiles. 'I know you will, Nurse Cook. Now I want you to keep your exam results to yourself until the other girls are told.'

'I'd love to know if Annette — I mean, Nurse Turney, has passed.'

'I'm sure you would. But I've told you all you should know.'

Resuming her fierce Matron expression, the august lady marched to the door saying, 'I will ring your mother, and an ambulance will take you home

— when your mother is ready for you.'

Katherine lay back on her pillow dazed. Feeling both happy to have done so brilliantly in her exams and to be going home for an extended holiday, but sad to be in pain and unable to work.

Then there was her broken bike.

And Martin — what an infuriating man he was. He'd stolen her heart, like the popular song said — and left her wondering why he kept letting her down.

He was kind and thoughtful in one sense — and yet she had to share him with his mother. And that she would not do. She wanted to come first, not far down on the list of his commitments.

Should she ease herself away from him? Find a boyfriend who not only put her first, but also one she could rely on?

But the problem was, she loved Martin Holt. And was she being as possessive as she was accusing his mother of being? She gave a little laugh to think she might be!

And she couldn't ignore him because Martin was the only one she could ask to have her bicycle mended. And she'd already asked him to lend her money to pay the vet bill. Which reminded her of the injured dog in the vet surgery. Was it making progress after its operation she wondered?

And then there was Gerry Mitchell. A known thief she'd been told. He'd made himself a nuisance during his National Service too, and was thrown out of the Army. And then she thought of her dad, giving his life for his country, suffering to win the war, and Gerry complaining because he didn't like the army food and discipline after the war.

He reminded Katherine of those few nurses who couldn't take the hospital discipline, who complained constantly, didn't pull their weight, leaving the other nurses to do much of their work.

Unfortunately, Gerry seemed to have thrived. His car and swanky clothes, were evidence of his success — or of his criminal ways.

But the worst thing, as far as she knew, was he was still hoping she would go out with him.

Katherine shuddered.

Another knock sounded on the door and in walked Annette.

'Hello.' Katherine said weakly. She felt frail.

Annette smiled to see her friend in bed and asked, 'What on earth has happened to you?'

'I fell off my bicycle. I stupidly had my head down because it was raining — and ran into a bus!'

'Oh dear Katherine, it looks as if you have too. Your face is bruised. '

'Is it?'

Annette picked up her make up mirror from her dressing table and gave it to Katherine. 'Take a look.'

Katherine grimaced to see the small cut on her cheek and the swelling and dark patches which had developed on her face. 'Ugh! It's just as well I can't go into the wards. I might make the patients feel worse. That's why Matron is sending me home.'

'Lucky you.'

Katherine was bursting to tell her friend the good news about her exam result. But had to avoid saying anything about it. She said, 'I'm not exactly lucky. I've a few other minor injuries — like a fractured arm.'

'That don't sound minor to me.'

'They don't feel minor either!'

Annette laughed. But Katherine found her sore face only allowed her to make a crooked smile.

'Oh, I have a message from reception to deliver to you.' Annette took out an envelope from her pocket and gave it to Katherine.

It had her name on it, and it was written by Martin.

It's his excuse for not coming to pick me up, thought Katherine. I wouldn't be in this mess if he'd been on time and taken me to the hospital on time.

'Aren't you going to open it?'

'I know what it is, Annette.'

Annette sat down on the corner of her bed saying, 'Can I do anything for you?'

'If you have the time you could pack a few things for me, if you would. I don't know what time the ambulance is coming to take me home, but I feel I can't get my case down from the top of the wardrobe, let alone put anything in it.'

Giving Annette directions to find her case and to pack some things from her drawer in it, took a while. Katherine began to feel worse, rather then better, but grateful for the help she was getting.

She thought Matron was right to send her home. She wanted to be away from everyone — except her Mum — for a while.

Annette remarked on her shoes. 'How many shoes do you want to take home with you?'

'None. Thank you. I've plenty of pairs at home.'

'How many have you got?'

'Thirty at the last count.'

'Have you that many? I only have three pairs of shoes to my name — and one pair are my bedroom slippers.'

Katherine explained, 'I'm a shoe collector.'

'That's right. I remember you saying you salvaged shoes. I envy you wearing some I've seen you wearing.'

You wouldn't like to be in my shoes, Katherine thought bitterly.

'Oh by the way, Katherine, I almost forgot to tell you. That ex patient, Gerry Mitchell, has been asking after you.'

Katherine almost screamed. She wished she'd told Annette about Gerry so that Annette would know to avoid him — and certainly not speak to him.

But now it was too late.

Trying to look unconcerned Katherine asked, 'What did he say?'

'He wanted to know what duty roster you were on.'

'Did you tell him?'

Annette looked at her friend, 'I said I didn't know. He said he would find out from another nurse.'

Katherine closed her eyes. She wanted to know what else the wretched man had said, but hoped Annette, and the other nurses he might have spoken to knew she didn't like him and had been dismissive.

Annette said, 'I can see you need to be left in peace.' She'd finished packing and closed the suitcase.

'Thanks for coming. And for packing my things.'

'Look after yourself and get better quickly,' her friend said slipping out of the room.

As soon as Annette had wished her well and left, Katherine opened Martin's letter and read it.

Dear Katherine

I'm very sorry to hear about your accident, and hope you will soon feel better.

Your mother was very hospitable,

but she delayed me — I was dismayed to find you'd gone before I got back. I brought a tin of cakes for you from your mother, but I thought you wouldn't mind if Tom and I ate them as I was told you will be going home to recover from your injuries, and no doubt she will make you some more.

I'll be in touch soon.
Love,
Martin.

Well, thought Katherine, after reading the note. He's probably telling the truth. He would not find it difficult to chat to her mum, who was a chatterbox. But he seemed to see her mother's company more important than hers. He could, she thought, easily have said he'd just popped in to collect some clothes for me then rushed off again.

But no, he'd stayed and chatted, while she'd waited, biting her nails for him to return. Then after she realised she'd be late for work, she leaped on her bicycle, and rode head down into a bus.

Now look at the state of her — and it was all his fault!

Suddenly Katherine chuckled because she knew he shouldn't be blamed for everything — but she felt sandwiched between two mothers! His, and hers.

★ ★ ★

When Katherine arrived home, her mother was concerned to see her battered body, but knew from Matron's letter that she would soon recover.

Her mum loved having her daughter, Kitty, at home again, and enjoyed preparing the meals she liked.

The next day the postman delivered a surprising heap of get well cards from her friends which decorated the mantelpiece. But not one from Martin. He was enjoying her cake!

One evening the phone rang.

Mum went to answer it and seemed to be ages chattering.

Katherine thought it must me one of Mum's friends, but eventually she came back and said, 'Kitty, it's that gentleman, Martin Holt, wanting to speak to you.'

Katherine walked into the hall and picked up the receiver. 'Hello, Martin,' she said rather woodenly.

'How are you?'

'As you would expect after crashing into a bus.'

'I hoped you were feeling better.'

'You hope in vain.'

'Would it help if I picked you up tomorrow and we went over to see my mother, she's dying to see you?'

Katherine's blood seemed to boil. 'No, it would not.'

'Oh, well, another time perhaps.'

The devil had got into Katherine. She said in a raised voice, 'I have no wish to meet your mother.'

She heard him draw in his breath. He was silent for a few moments. Then he said, 'If that is so, you need say no more. But you may not know that I collected your injured dog from the vet's and took him over to my mother's house this morning. She sent me out immediately to buy a dog's bed, collar and lead, a brush — and some dog food too of course. She seems happy to keep him.'

What Katherine should have said, was that his mother was kind to have taken the dog in. Instead, she thought it was typical for his mother to have told Martin to collect some bedding and food for the dog. And, like a good boy, he had trotted out and done as he was told. She said sarcastically, 'I hope your mother will allow you to walk the dog.'

'Oh yes, I will be expected to go for a walk with her and the dog occasionally.'

Katherine took several deep breaths and blurted out, 'So what are you allowed to do on your own? Name the dog?'

It was so rude of her that she wasn't surprised that Martin said curtly, 'I hope you will soon feel better,' as he quietly put down the receiver. Just like his mother, thought Katherine.

As soon as he'd rung off Katherine felt dreadful. She'd been downright mean. She felt sure she'd never see Martin again after making him angry.

It was a tragedy of her own making. How could she have been so bad-mannered to a man who'd gone out of his way to help her?

Katherine deserved to lose the man she loved because she'd kicked him in the teeth — all because she was jealous of his mother!

An Unexpected Visitor

It took Katherine several days for her injuries to improve. And she was fighting her own low spirits. Her mother looked after her very well, but Katherine was not used to being idle after her busy life at the hospital.

She had too much time to think about Martin, and how stupid she'd been to have lost her temper — and she had lost him too — by being critical of his mother and unfair to him. She had too much time to feel sorry for herself.

'Kitty, love, I think we should take a walk into town this fine morning,' Margaret Cook suggested, trying to cheer her up. 'It's market day and a lovely warm summer's day. Going over the bridge the river always looks a picture at this time of the year, with the green trees and meadows either side. I like to see the wild geese there feeding.'

Katherine knew she needed to pull herself together. As a nurse, she knew a patient needed to play their part in recovery to health.

'Mum, I'd like too,' she said getting out of the armchair, 'I can't walk fast but the exercise will do me good.'

Her mother beamed at her. 'I'm sure it'll make you feel better. And we can catch the bus back if you are feeling a bit wobbly.'

'I'm not that much of an invalid!'

Her mother smiled, glad to see her daughter's spirit returned.

Returning her smile back, Katherine felt her father would be proud of her mother. Margaret kept herself fit by housework and walking into town — even if she had to take the bus back with her heavy shopping.

And she kept happy, although living on an army widow's pension wasn't always easy. She got out to play bingo in the wintertime, and outdoor bowls in the summer, and enjoyed going to the cinema once a week with her friends.

They didn't need to put coats on — the weather was so mild.

'We can look around the market and I'll nip in the butchers on the way back and get some chicken pieces for our lunch,' Margaret said, her mind on keeping her patient well fed.

Katherine went upstairs to get her purse, because she'd thought she might need to take the bus home if she felt too tired to walk there and back.

* * *

By the time she was outside the house and walking Katherine felt elated. Going into town was the right thing to do. Her mother chatted all the time, but it was nice for mother and daughter to be together.

The old stone built town of Stamford was always interesting to see — when you had the time, and at present, Katherine had plenty of time to look about and admire its beauty. In fact, as they approached the town there was a huge decorative notice, which bid visitors to, 'Stay awhile amidst its ancient charms.'

It took you back in history to medieval times with its timbered houses and many churches. And in more recent times, when the city was a stop for people travelling by coach to the north of England, the old George Hotel, a stage coach inn, was still there.

When the railways took over from the horse-drawn carriages, the main line north went through nearby Peterborough, and Stamford avoided being rebuilt, so it remained as was, a charming old market town.

Up High Street St Margaret's, past The George, Katherine didn't feel a twinge of pain from her injuries.

'You know, Mum, I think I'm fully recovered. I'll have to ring Matron and see if she'll have me back.'

'Not while your arm's still in a sling, she won't let you near the wards.'

Katherine pressed her lips together,

knowing nurses were often advising patients to take it easy after an accident and not to rush back into their normal activities without giving their body time to heal properly.

And after they had reached the town centre, Katherine had changed her mind, because she began to feel a little weary.

Then they met one of Margaret's friends, Mrs Blackwell, now out of hospital and full of praise for the medical treatment she'd been given. She made Katherine blush when she was gushing with praise for her work there too.

'Everyone likes her there, Margaret,' said Mrs Blackwell, 'they say she's an outstandingly good nurse.'

'I'm glad Kitty is a natural nurse,' said her mother looking at her daughter proudly.

Hearing her mother call her, Kitty, and knowing the hospital called her Katherine, was a secret, Mrs Blackwell winked at her.

'I like the work,' Katherine said, 'although it's very hard at times.'

'I should say, it is,' Mrs Blackwell agreed, she liked to repeat what she said, again and again, 'They think ever so highly of her in the hospital. All the nurses spoke well of her. And the doctors. She was nipping about doing this and that all the time . . . and what a shame she'd hurt her arm. How did that happen?'

Of course, Mrs Blackwell wanted to know all about how it happened, and then the two women began to chatter about people she didn't know — so soon Katherine began to feel bored.

And her injuries ached as she stood there waiting for the women to finish their never-ending conversation.

'Mum,' she said at last, when there was a lull in the conversion, 'Do you mind if I take the bus home? I'm beginning to feel a bit exhausted.'

'Yes, of course you can, Kitty love.' Mrs Cook looked at her watch. 'There's one in a quarter-of-an-hour. Have you

173

got your house key in case you get home before me?'

'I have, Mum,' Katherine replied after checking in her purse.

Leaving the women still gossiping, Katherine made her way to the bus station, hoping the bus was there waiting so she could sit down.

It wasn't, and Katherine walked up and down until the bus came at last. Katherine clambered on and sat down thankfully.

Sitting on the bus Katherine's mind turned to Martin Holt, and to the disgraceful way she'd treated him — after he'd been so kind to her. After all, did it matter if his mother was over protective? She knew Mrs Holt was a widow — like her mum — and Katherine knew her mum thought the world of her.

Mothers were inclined to be watchful over their chicks.

And grown children could be just as solicitous of their older parents. It was nice that they were. She'd been much too hasty to condemn Martin's care for his mother — especially as she'd never even met the women.

Maybe Mrs Holt's bark was worse than her bite?

* * *

Daydreaming, Katherine got off the bus and began walking towards home when she got a nasty shock.

Ex-patient and bully, Gerry Mitchell, had parked his car right outside the house!

Katherine gasped. He was obviously waiting for her.

Seeing his cocky profile, with a cigarette hanging out of his mouth as he sat in the driving seat, she was filled with terror.

He must have discovered she was out and he was waiting for her to return.

Hurriedly, she retraced her steps wondering where she could go. She couldn't ask Martin to help her anymore — he would probably tell her to get lost if she rang him asking for his assistance again.

Blind with the tears that had come into her eyes, Katherine walked quickly away as far as she could and then rested her back against the rough bark of an old oak tree, panting.

She was in deep trouble. Her heart was drumming away inside her chest.

Where could she go? Mrs Blackwell's house was the nearest, but Mrs Blackwell was in town with her mother.

She could get the bus back into town, but she would have to go and wait at the bus stop on the main road and then it would be easy for Gerry to find her. Anyway, she didn't know when the next bus was due — until she saw the bus timetable which was at the bus stop.

So where could she hide? She was already sore and feeling very tired. She badly wanted to go home and put her feet up, but that wretched man was blocking her way.

She'd have to wait for Mum to come

back from town — or was Mum already in the house?

Katherine shook herself. She knew she was in a right state. And she shouldn't go on allowing his man to ruin her life. Gerry Mitchell had an evil streak in him.

Martin had told her Gerry had been kicked out of the army. Now he'd managed to amass enough money to buy himself expensive Teddy Boy clothes and a new car — and yet he worked in a bakery. Unless his parents — or someone else — had given him the money for his showy things, where had he got them all from?

Martin had told her he'd found out how Gerry Mitchell managed to get what he wanted in life.

But he was not going to get her!

Suddenly she knew she had to deal with the difficulty herself, make a decision — overcome the problem, once and for all. She was training to be a nurse, which involved dealing with people — and some could be difficult.

So why did she need to be worried sick about Gerry? True, he was following her — which wasn't pleasant, but he must have been told by now that she was going out with Martin, although she hadn't seen much of him recently.

But today as he'd turned up, she wondered if Gerry knew she'd had a quarrel with Martin?

However, Katherine felt she shouldn't continue to let her life be spoilt by a blackmailer. She knew Matron already suspected Mr Mitchell had started the fire, so even if he went and reported her to Matron, she knew that Katherine didn't smoke.

Katherine decided she wouldn't put up with being persecuted any longer. She would have to do something — right now.

Katherine remembered the last time, when Matron had arrived as Gerry was talking to her, she noticed he'd disappeared quickly. Gerry obviously didn't want to be confronted with the strong character Matron was. So it seemed Gerry was a coward — as often bullies were.

But how could she frighten him away?

She just must think of something. Fast.

Courage was needed. The courage her late dad had possessed. Katherine would confront Gerry and tell him straight that, however much he may want her to, she would not go out with him. Ever.

Walking towards the house she noticed Gerry jumped to attention and throwing his cigarette on the pavement he screwed it down with his foot.

'Ah, there you are at last,' he said lifting his chin in his cocky way. 'I knew you'd be coming sooner or later.'

Katherine lifted her chin too. 'Hello, Mr Mitchell, what do you want?'

'As if you don't know.'

Katherine stood her ground. If she could be impolite to Martin, she could certainly be rude to this man she found offensive. 'No, I don't know why you keep pestering me. I understand the police are interested in you Mr Mitchell — I am certainly not.'

Although she herself was shaking, Katherine was pleased to see her boldness had unsettled her adversary.

For the first time she saw he was alarmed within himself. He obviously had a guilty conscience about something. And her mentioning the police had clearly upset him.

She rejoiced knowing she'd successfully got the better of him.

'Perhaps some other day,' he muttered.

Katherine heard another car motoring along the road and turned to watch it, as it slowed to park near her house. Curious to know who it could be, Katherine moved nearer to recognise with joy that it was Martin's car. He got out, and not seeing her, he strode to the front door and rang the bell, then he stood waiting there.

Katherine felt she wanted to run to

him, but he turned when he saw her, said, 'Good morning,' and went back to his car, opened his boot, and took out her bicycle. It was mended, cleaned up, and looking brand new.

'Oh, Martin,' she cried walking towards him as fast as she could, 'You have brought my bicycle back. Mended. How very kind of you!'

He seemed a little surprised to see her. 'I'm glad to see you up and about,' he said rather neutrally.

She was near him now, and noticed Gerry and his car had gone. She said, 'I've just come back from town and I'm ready to drop, can you come in a moment so that I can talk to you?'

He looked at her challengingly. 'As long as your mother isn't there. She talks the hind leg of a horse — and I'm in a hurry to get back to the office.'

Katherine was amazed. Now they were equal. He'd been just as critical of her mother as she'd been about his. 'She hasn't come back from town yet,' she answered.

Opening the garden gate she said, 'Would you be so kind as to wheel my bicycle to the shed for me?' as if she were asking Jack the porter to do something on the hospital ward.

He could see she still had her arm in a sling, so he put the bike in the shed. But he didn't ask how she was which surprised Katherine. He seemed to want to deliver the bicycle and be gone.

Unlocking the back door she said, 'Please come in the kitchen a minute.'

Closing the shed door with her bike safely inside, he looked at his watch, and said abruptly, as if he was speaking to a client, 'I only have a minute.'

She was going to apologise for being so rude to him, but he was not being exactly friendly with her, so after she had let him into the kitchen she accepted he was annoyed with her and said, 'I'm afraid I can't afford to pay you for all I owe you. But I can give you something each month.' She took out her purse and offered him her last ten shilling note.

'Keep it,' he said abruptly. 'You don't owe me anything, Katherine.' Turning his back on her quickly he let himself out of the house.

He didn't give her a chance to say how sorry she was for being so unfair about his mother. Or to show she wanted to repair the rift between them.

He didn't reply, or turn back to wave at her, when she followed him and called out, 'Goodbye, and thank you again for bringing my bike back.'

Watching him drive away Katherine felt devastated. It was clear she'd well and truly lost the man she loved

She went back into the house and sat down at the kitchen table, and sobbed.

Matron Learns The Truth

Annette phoned her next day. 'Katherine,' she said, 'I have some good news — and some not so good news to tell you.'

Katherine felt she needed lifting when she replied, 'Tell me the good news first, please.'

Annette sounded thrilled when she said, 'Believe it or not, I came second in our set, after you, in our exams.'

Katherine was overjoyed and squealed, 'Well done!'

'I couldn't believe it at first, I thought someone had made a mistake, I don't mean you coming first, I mean me coming second on the list. Of course it won't be such a surprise for you, Katherine, as you always do come top . . . but for me to be up there is absolutely unbelievable.'

'I'm pleased for us both.'

'I'm over the moon, but you sound a little subdued.'

'I did know my result,' confessed Katherine, 'Matron told me before I came home. But she said I was to keep it to myself, that's why I didn't tell you. But she wouldn't tell me yours. So I'm very happy for you. You deserve it because you've had such a struggle learning the stuff.'

'You helped me a lot, Katherine, so you must take some of the credit for it.'

'Your parents must be thrilled.'

'They are.'

Katherine gave a great sigh of relief. 'Now we have passed our second year state exams we are third year students. One year more before we take the big one, our State Registered Nursing Certificate.'

Annette gave a cough.

'What's the matter? Now you've proved you done so well in your nursing exams, you should pass your SRN.'

Annette gave a loud sigh. 'It isn't studying that bothers me now.'

'Oh? What is it then?' Katherine braced herself to hear the bad news.

Annette said, 'I confessed to Matron that you had helped me study for my exams and it was largely due to you that I had done so well.'

Katherine blushed. 'You shouldn't have said that. You did all the work, Annette. I merely encouraged you. You'd would have done the same for me if I'd wanted your help.'

'Anyway, while I was with Matron I then told her that I'd been cowardly, and had not admitted to being in the linen room and smoking there, and that although I was always careful to put out my cigarette I may not have, and started the fire.'

Katherine tutted. 'What on earth did you tell her that for? The fire is over, forgotten.'

'Because I told Matron that you knew I was keeping it a secret, and I thought I had put a tremendous burden on your shoulders. You've been unhappy since then, and have shown signs of stress.

And it's all my fault for being so cowardly and not owning up. I said I believed that's why you had your accident.'

'Oh, dear me, Annette. What did she say?'

'I got a long lecture about a nurse's duties and responsibilities. She asked me, what if I had given a patient the wrong drug, was it right that we should cover it up?

'I said that you and I had decided as no harm had been done, it was better not to say anything.'

'What did she say to that?'

Annette replied, 'She wasn't too pleased. She said we should have come to her and let her make the judgement on that.'

Katherine knew the whole business was more complicated than Annette knew, but she didn't tell her about Gerry Mitchell. She asked, 'So what did Matron decide to do?'

'She told me to go back on duty. She said she would speak to you when you were better.'

Katherine gave a shiver. It made going back to work seem less inviting.

She grimaced and said to Annette, 'Well as least you've got it off your chest. And I don't think you need to worry anymore.'

'Well I do feel relieved to have told Matron. But I'm still worried about you, Katherine, because I don't think you are out of the woods yet.'

'Yes, I am upset, but it has nothing to do with the fire. I broke up with Martin — you know, Jack the porter.'

'Oh, no!'

'Yes. Unfortunately.' Katherine then felt she wanted to admit it was her fault so she related how the quarrel started, and how she'd been rude about his mother. She ended by saying, 'I feel so embarrassed about what I said to him about his mother now.'

Annette sighed. 'Oh, I am sorry to hear it. It's not like you to be like that.'

'Well, I was. Really awful, making it clear I didn't like his mother. Mind you, she did lie to me about him being away, when he wasn't. So I told him I didn't want to meet her, and that he was a mother's boy. Martin didn't like it — in fact he walked out on me.'

'Oh dear!'

'Can't be helped,' Katherine said as lightly as she could, but knowing she could have avoided it. 'I'll get over it. Especially when I'm back at work and haven't time to brood over it.'

Katherine said that, but deep in her heart she knew that wasn't true. She would regret losing Martin all her life.

⋆   ⋆   ⋆

The day Katherine went back to the hospital for a check up she was cheered to find the nurses' doctor had good news for her.

'All your injuries have healed nicely,' he said, 'but I think you should be on light duties on the ward for a fortnight before you use that arm.'

Katherine smiled. It was not only marvellous to be allowed back working again — she wouldn't have too much time to mope about Martin.

But the smile was soon removed from her face after the doctor said, 'Go and see Matron and give her this report, will you, Nurse?'

Katherine was apprehensive because of what Annette had told her a few days ago. And after what Annette said Katherine had written to Matron admitting her part in the cover up.

★   ★   ★

To her surprise Matron greeted her with a stiff smile. 'Sit down, Nurse Cook,' she said, 'I'm pleased to see you back here.'

She took the report the doctor had given Katherine for her and going to her desk she sat down and opened it and read it while Katherine waited.

'Now, Nurse,' Matron said, snapping the folder closed and putting it down in front of her. 'How are you feeling?'

'Definitely much better, thank you, Matron.'

'The doctor wants you on light duties for a while, and I think we could place you in the TB facility for a stint — where you won't have so much physical work to do.'

'Thank you, Matron.'

Matron sat back on her chair and regarded Katherine thoughtfully. 'Now about the other matter . . . '

Katherine blinked and wriggled her toes in her shoes, wishing she were elsewhere.

After studying her Matron said, 'It is always better to tell the truth, and I hope you will make up your mind to do that when I ask you again to think back to the day there was a fire in the linen room.'

Katherine couldn't bear looking at Matron's shiny glasses and looked down at her hands on her lap.

'Do you think Nurse Turney was responsible for the fire?'

Katherine took a deep breath in and said, 'I honestly don't know. I suppose she could have . . . but — '

'You told me you thought it could have been a patient.'

'Yes, that is more likely.'

'Which patient do you think it may have been, smoking in the linen room?'

'Matron, it was a long time ago. I can't remember.'

'I think you can. What about Mr Mitchell, I saw you talking to outside the Nurses' Home not long ago? Are you going out with him? I understand he's be asking after you.'

Katherine couldn't deny that. She squeezed her hands together and said, 'I don't like him, Matron, he's been a nuisance, harassing me.'

'So I understand.'

After a pause, Katherine added, 'He's blaming me for the fire — although I don't smoke.'

'Ah, now we are getting nearer to the truth. Do you think he mistook you for Nurse Turney — you look very alike in your uniform?'

'Yes, Matron.'

She seemed to have worked it out, so there was no need for Katherine to hide anything now. Katherine waited.

At last Matron spoke. 'I think Mr Mitchell could well have started the fire and wanted to put the blame on one of the nurses.'

Katherine nodded in agreement. 'I know he smokes — like a chimney.'

Matron gave a wry smile. 'And what about Mr Mitchell's character?'

'Untrustworthy,' Katherine answered at once. 'He's a bully — and a thief, so Martin — I mean, Jack the porter, told me.'

Matron smiled as she took out another folder from her desk drawer. 'Now I am building up a picture of what really happened. Don't look so worried, Nurse Cook, I'm not angry with you. I think you've been exceedingly brave, and a loyal friend to a fellow nurse. But . . .'

Katherine looked at the senior nurse hopefully.

Matron continued, ' . . . the whole episode has made you unhappy and we can't have that. Can we?'

'No, Matron,' said Katherine. But her unhappiness had little to do with the fire — or Gerry Mitchell.

It had everything to do with her relationship with Martin Holt which had been broken. And Matron might be able to shake the truth out of her nurses, and to help mend broken bones, but she couldn't mend broken hearts.

Katherine would have to do something about that herself.

'Matron,' she said, 'Annette and I are overjoyed we've both done well in our second year exams and we intend to study hard to get our State Registered Nurse qualification..'

'Good,' murmured Matron.

'But,' said Katherine encouraged by Matron's wide smile, 'I still have a problem with Mr Mitchell who seems to think I like him and I do not.'

Matron looked over her glasses at her and said, 'I knew he had a police record when he came here as a patient. But I don't normally discuss a patient's circumstances with my nurses because as far as nurses are concerned, they are just sick people who need to be looked after until they recover.

'But, if they cause trouble — and in this case I think Mr Mitchell probably did cause the fire — then I can only report my suspicion to the police. But my duty is to care for my nurses. For you, in this case, because you are being bothered by him. And I will inform the police about his behaviour. That should put a stop to him pestering you.'

'Thank you, Matron,' Katherine said, feeling a huge weight being lifted from her spirits.

'However, you should have told me about this a long time ago and then you would not have had to suffer it for so long.'

'Yes, Matron.'

'Now run along, I have a lot of work to do.'

Katherine was smiling as she left Matron's office — yet only half her difficulties were over.

Life Goes On

Katherine was determined to throw herself into her work and to forget about Martin — as far as she could.

Being a third year student nurse meant more responsibilities, and even helping the youngest nurses who'd just joined the hospital. It made Katherine and Annette feel they had learned a lot, and grown up, since they had arrived as newcomers to their profession of caring for the sick.

Annette blossomed and was no longer like the frightened kitten she used to be.

But Katherine, much as she tried to overcome her heartache, couldn't feel relaxed. Martin kept haunting her in much the same way that Gerry Mitchell used to. She hadn't seen either of them for months and was grateful Gerry was not around. But she was not happy Martin kept away.

She looked anxiously at the morning post every day to see if there was a letter from him. She jumped when the phone rang — wondering, was it Martin?

'It's ridiculous!' she told herself as she was showing a young nurse how to fold the corner of a sheet and tuck it in.

'What is?' the first year nurse who'd only just come onto the ward asked in a scared voice.

Katherine smiled and said, 'Not you, nurse, I am.'

'You are very competent. Sister told me. One of the best nurses. That's why she put me to work with you.'

Katherine replied, 'That was kind of Sister to say that because she is qualified, and knows much more than I do. But at present my mind is not on bed-making. I'm thinking about what I have done far away from the hospital.'

The young nurse nodded. 'Boyfriend trouble?'

Katherine replied, 'How did you guess?'

'Your faraway look.'

Sister came walking by and snapped, 'Hurry up, you two. You shouldn't be taking all day to make one bed. There are six more for you to make. And I've a patient coming up from surgery who will be needing attention at any moment. I'll need you to help give out the meals when the trolley comes up from the kitchen too.'

'Yes, Sister,' the student nurses chorused in unison.

Katherine made the effort to concentrate on the job at hand — as she'd been trying to do for weeks.

But she found it impossible not to slip into thinking about Martin. He just would not remove himself from her mind.

* * *

Katherine was not the only one pining. Martin had been too.

Visiting his mother the previous week he'd been greeted by an exuberant young dog, who made him feel thankful he'd helped it recover as he picked it up to stroke it and was licked all over.

His mother's house looked a little less pristine than it was on his last visit. Dog toys lay about and there was a snug dog basket in the kitchen.

'What do you call this little brute?' he asked placing the dog down on the floor.

'Kim,' replied his mother, looking at the dog fondly.

'I gather his leg is mended?'

'I took him to the vet yesterday, and he said it was.'

Martin didn't have to ask if she intended to keep Kim. Kim was clearly at home. And his mother was well occupied looking after the little animal. Martin sighed with relief. She had a companion and wouldn't be asking him to move back.

'So how are you getting on?' his

mother asked as she prepared a simple salad for lunch.

'Very well, thank you.'

His mother gave him a knowing look. 'Well, I would say only fairly well. You have the air of a harassed man.'

'No, I'm not in the least harassed. My job is going well. I've several new clients I like — which is a blessing. And I enjoy my rugby.'

'It's a rough game.'

'So it is. That's probably why I enjoy it. A bit of a tumble keeps me fit — and it gets rid of my aggression too.'

'Aggression?' His mother held up the knife she was slicing the cucumber with.

'Certainly. I get mad at times and it soothes me down.'

'So what is bothering you at present?'

'I must find a house. I can't go on living with Tom forever.'

Putting the slices of cucumber on the two plates and topping the salad with a dollop of mayonnaise, Valerie said, 'I wouldn't have thought that would be an interesting exercise for you, finding a new home. Pour yourself a beer will you?'

Martin helped himself to a drink saying, 'I just can't make up my mind.'

'Would you like me to help you?'

'No . . . no thank you.'

Taking the plates into the dining room his mother looked at him quizzically. 'I suppose it's because you want your future bride to choose a house with you?'

Martin ignored that remark and bit into his bread roll.

'You won't solve the problem by ignoring it,' his mother said after a minute's silence.

Martin put down his knife and fork with a clatter. 'What problem?' he asked, trying to look innocent.

'Your girl.'

'I'm not marrying Jilly Masters, if that's what you think.'

His mother smiled at him a little sadly, 'You know very well who I mean.

You've had a quarrel with her, I can tell.'

Martin felt unable to finish his meal.

'Why don't you bring your nurse here? I've met her and think she's a lovely girl.'

Martin choked as he tried to sip his beer. He looked at his mother pointedly, 'You've met her? When?'

Valerie's eyes twinkled as she told him all about how she'd met Katherine Cook at the auction. And their lively discussion about shoes.

A Chance To Talk

Later that day, Martin left his mother's home in a daze. He meant to go back to the office and finish off some work he'd been doing, but he hadn't the heart to do it. All he could think about was, Katherine, who his mother had found so charming — and she was so right for him, she'd said.

Only it had been a bit one sided, because Katherine had made it clear she didn't like his mother. So how was he going to persuade her?

His mind was constantly thinking of Katherine and her sweet, gentle nature. And he hadn't taken the opportunity to make his feelings for her clear. He could so easily have said he loved her.

Now, trying to get back to the way they were, might be difficult. She'd made no attempt to get in touch with him since he'd taken her bike back, when she'd looked very tense — as if she'd seen a ghost — and he hadn't helped matters by being short with her.

Although she had been pretty unflattering about his mother, and saying he was under her thumb.

The truth was, both he and Katherine had lost their tempers. He'd said things about her sweet, chatty, mother he now regretted — just as she had said things about his mother she now probably regretted. They really shouldn't have split up over a few harsh words.

He needed to buy a house, settle his future with Katherine, the girl he loved.

But how was he going to repair the damage? He knew Katherine was a stubborn woman, a nurse had to be tough as well as kind. He should have apologised, and set the matter straight days ago, and now weeks had gone by . . .

He was pleased when he thought it was rugby practice that evening, because a good run around, and a scrum or two would help him to work off his frustration — and maybe help him to think of the best way to approach Katherine.

But when he got to the Rugby Club and met the lads, their loud, rough jokes and camaraderie did nothing to dispel his gloom. He found he still couldn't forget Katherine and concentrate on the exercises — or the friendly game afterwards.

'Martin, get your finger out — run man,' he vaguely heard the coach shouting at him.

But all he could think about how he would explain to Katherine that he was still trying to help her, because he loved her. He had made sure she was no longer being frightened by Gerry Mitchell too.

He'd been to the bakery where Gerry Mitchell worked. He'd met the easy going manager, offering to check his accounts free of charge, explaining that he was an accountant and the police were anxious to know if Mr Mitchell had been helping himself to the bakery's profits.

Martin found he had. And Gerry Mitchell, when accused of theft, thought he was talking to Jack the hospital porter, and told him, behind his hand, that he'd been clever to siphon off hundreds of pounds for his private use. He'd boasted that he'd managed to get, 'Some togs to impress the girls. And a Hillman car.'

When the manager overheard Gerry Mitchell boasting about the way he'd been cheated of his profits, he was fuming, and offered to be a witness in court.

Martin remembered feeling delighted to see Gerry being caught so easily and facing trial — which would keep him away from Katherine.

He just had to find a way to tell Katherine the good news . . .

Martin didn't notice an eighteen-stone rugby player running fast towards him and butting him before he could move out of the way. The impact of falling badly, resulting in a jarring crack in his knee — made Martin holler in agony.

'Call an ambulance!' Martin heard a man shout before he fainted.

* * *

'Nurse Cook,' Katherine heard her name being called and walked back to hear what the ward Sister had to say.

'There's been a call from Casualty. A man has been brought in after a sports accident and they are short of nurses. Will you go along there and help out until the night staff arrive?'

Katherine could have said, no, I'm on light duties, and can't help lift a heavy patient or move trolleys around. But Katherine wasn't one to avoid a call for help, and she thought she could comfort the patient if nothing else.

'Yes, Sister, I'll go right away.'

She could ride her bike now and was thankful Martin had had it mended for her as she rode along to the Casualty department. It was embarrassing he wouldn't accept payment for it. Or for the vet fees — but as his mother had taken the little dog that didn't matter as much. She would like to have seen the dog again. But it was nice to know it had a good home. Because as much as she had criticised Martin's mother, she felt sure she would provide a comfortable home for the animal she'd rescued.

★ ★ ★

Arriving at Casualty, she was soon swept into the work necessary to deal with an injured person who'd just been brought in.

Sister told her, 'The patient is, believe it or not, Jack. Do you remember our ex-porter?'

Katherine gave a little gasp. 'Yes, indeed I do, Sister.' Was it really Martin?

Fortunately the nurse didn't notice Katherine's flaming cheeks.

Sister went on, 'He's a nice chap, is Jack, was always good humoured, but he's not very chirpy at the moment. His knee's been damaged — a sport's injury — and I expect he'll need an operation to set it right. Prepare a drip for him, will you, Nurse?'

'Yes, Sister,' nodded Katherine, keen to be of assistance right away.

Waiting for a doctor to come to treat Martin, Katherine felt as if she was the suffering patient whose leg had to be manipulated back into its correct position.

'He'll need a wash, Nurse,' Sister told her. 'He looks as if he's been rolling around in the mud.'

Katherine went to fetch a bowl of water and a wash cloth, and was told by Sister when she got back. 'I've got a child who's got to have her stomach pumped because she swallowed some moth balls thinking they were sweets, so I'm going to leave you to look after this patient.'

Katherine felt pleased to think her years of nursing had given her expertise that was useful.

But what made her almost drop the bowl of water she was carrying, as if she was an inexperienced nurse, was seeing the patient's pained expression and the unnatural position of his limb as he lay groaning behind the curtains.

'Hello Martin,' she managed to say softly as she put down the bowl.

'Katherine!' His grey colour and the strain on his face suddenly became animated by his attempt to smile.

'Goodness me. Whatever happened to you?'

'I was playing rugby — and was felled by a charging bull.'

'It looks as if he sat on you too.'

'He did land on my knee. It's damned painful.'

Katherine rinsed the cloth in the warm water then began to wipe the blood off his face. 'Mmm, I can see you are in pain,' she said sympathetically, because it wasn't long ago she'd been in an accident herself and knew how it could hurt. Noting his grubby rugby shirt and shorts she wondered how she was going to get them off, thinking perhaps the doctor might assist her.

After she'd wiped his face, she tackled his arms and then his muddy knees being gentle so as not to jar the injured limb. Katherine, aware he was not comfortable, refrained from talking too much to him.

Then a doctor swept up and began his examination.

'Would you be kind enough to ring my mother,' he asked Katherine when the doctor had finished, 'and explain what has happened. Ask if I can come home for a while. Because I'll need someone to look after me. And please tell her not to worry.'

Katherine was the one who was worried, having to ring the woman. But she assured Martin she would do as he requested.

She was able to make him more comfortable as the painkillers began to ease his discomfort.

'Katherine,' he said taking her hand as the porter wheeled him into surgery,

'I've missed you. We ought to discuss things — I haven't been happy about us since . . . '

'Shush, Martin, you mustn't worry about that now.'

'But I must talk to you.'

Katherine replied, 'There are too many people about for us to talk here. Just lie back and when your surgery is over we can talk.'

'Do you promise?'

Katherine nodded. 'I promise.'

With a loud sigh Martin Holt lay back and Katherine watched as the surgery nurses took the trolley and wheeled it into the operation room.

She was confident the surgeon would be able to straighten out his limb and set the knee well. It was only a matter of time before Martin would be able to walk again.

'Nurse Cook.' She was wanted again to help with another patient. But Katherine didn't mind how much overtime she had to do. Looking after the sick was her vocation and she was happy to be of help to anyone who needed it.

But most of all she was happy to have the prospect of making it up with Martin. He did seem to be as anxious as she was that they become friends again.

She checked later to discover Martin had come out of surgery and was being sent to a ward where she knew the nurses were kind and experts at their job.

Katherine Listens To Her Feelings

It was almost eleven o'clock when Katherine was able to leave the hospital and go back to the Nurse's Home. It had been an exceptionally busy evening in Casualty, with an unusual number of people victims of accidents. Katherine had been able to assist the busy staff, and when she left she not only felt drained with tiredness, but satisfied she'd been useful too.

Martin had been given the best possible treatment — although she knew he wouldn't be feeling too happy. They'd given him a bed in Men's Surgical, and shooed away a group of his rugby-playing friends who'd come to see how he was, because they were too high-spirited, and he needed to rest.

She had only one worry now — she

should ring Mrs Holt before she collapsed into bed?

Katherine imagined Mrs Holt in bed with a cup of Ovaltine and being most irate if she was called to say her son had been in an accident and was in hospital.

But as she'd promised Martin she would ring her so she knew she must.

She had to wait while another nurse was using the phone in the lobby. And the nurse seemed to be gabbling for ages before Katherine was able to get to it.

Martin had given her his mother's number and she was on tenter hooks when Mrs Holt took so long to answer.

'Wansford, double-five-seven.'

Katherine recognised the way Mrs Holt answered the phone.

'I'm sorry to be so late in calling you. This is the hospital ringing, Mrs Holt. Your son, Martin, has had an accident on the rugby pitch. But he is all right. He's had minor surgery on his leg. He's going to make a good recovery.'

'Oh dear!' Katherine heard her say,

and went on quickly, 'he asks if he can be brought home to recover?'

'Of course he can. When? Right now?'

'Not tonight. The doctors will decide when, Mrs Holt.'

'I'll get his room dusted.'

Katherine was sure a little dust wouldn't matter. But then she remembered Matron was a great dust hater, so perhaps his mother wasn't such a fusspot.

'Will you ring the hospital tomorrow morning, Mrs Holt, after the surgeon has made his morning rounds?'

'Yes, I will. Thank you for letting me know. Give him my love will you?'

Katherine rang off quickly in case Mrs Holt thought of anything else — or recognised her voice.

Giving Martin the message, saying his mother had sent her love to him, wasn't going to be that easy. He was probably drugged and fast asleep after his treatment.

She would have to go and see him

tomorrow morning. And tomorrow was her day off and she had opportunity for asking for breakfast in bed. It only happened once a month, and she would miss it — what a shame. But duty to the sick came first, so Katherine resigned herself to going over to the Men's Surgical in the early morning to give Martin his mother's message.

In the morning Katherine felt strangely pleased to think that she was going to see Martin. She put on a skirt and twin set because she was off duty.

As she brushed her hair, looking in the mirror, she felt her hair looked attractive around her neck instead of being pinned up under her nurse's cap.

But she was nervous.

Martin may still be cross with her. The other nurses may tease her about going to see him on her day off, hinting they knew she was his girlfriend — and she wasn't any more. But perhaps their relationship, like his knee, could be repaired?

* * *

When she arrived at the ward and had been given permission by the Sister to speak to him, she found Martin was sitting up in bed eating his breakfast.

'Katherine!' he said quickly swallowing a mouthful of toast. 'How lovely to see you. Out of uniform too.'

'It's my day off.'

'Well that's nice of you to give me some of your precious time off duty. Have you come to give me another wash?' he asked mischievously.

Katherine smiled. 'Do you want me to?'

He laughed. 'Not now. I'll have one later when you're back on duty.'

She laughed seeing he was somewhat recovered, and she wasn't going to get away with giving him a quick few words from his mother.

'I rang your mother last night,' she said.

'Kind of you.'

'She is expecting you home when you

are discharged from the hospital . . . and she sends you her love.'

He was studying her closely as he said quietly, 'Thank you, Katherine.'

'Mind you,' she went on quickly, 'I don't know when you will be allowed home because I haven't seen what the doctor's diagnosis was. But you could ask him when he does his rounds later this morning.'

'I'll do that.'

'I must go. Sister only allowed me to come and give you your mother's message.'

'Please come back later.'

She looked into his eyes. He had the look of a man who'd had an accident, with a nasty bruise and swelling over one cheek and a cut lip. So, bearing in mind he was a patient and it was her duty to help him to get better, she didn't like to say no.

'If you are still here.'

'Then you must come over to Wansford and see me. If you come over by bus Mother will run you back.'

Katherine felt as if she'd been cut in two. There was a clear indication that he was not cross with her anymore. And that he wanted to see her again. But she wasn't sure if she wanted to be scrutinised by his mother.

Then she looked at him again and knew she still loved him. If she kept refusing to let him court her she might lose him forever and that would be her fault. Just because she'd formed an opinion that his mother ran his life, didn't mean it was true.

She knew lots of married people had difficulties with their mothers-in-law — and it was a familiar joke used by comedians.

But it wasn't a joke when it was a problem.

Surely she loved him enough to overcome her dislike of his mother?

Hadn't she enough strength of character to deal with it? Enough nursing training to understand his mother's point of view — to cope with a character she disliked? After all, his mother kept asking to see her, so she wasn't trying to put Martin off her.

Katherine took a deep breath in and said, 'I'd be pleased to come.'

Sister was marching down the ward towards her and Katherine said, 'I must go now before I get into Sister's bad books.'

With that she turned, but not before she saw him blow her a kiss.

She was walking on air as she left the ward. She knew Martin had forgiven her and they were friends again, so that when she brushed by Sister, who said, 'Your boyfriend will probably be going home today,' she didn't deny that Martin Holt was her boyfriend.

'She Can't Be That Bad'

Listless, Katherine wondered what she would do all day. She couldn't face studying. She hadn't any shopping to do — so she decided to go to the auction rooms.

It was her favourite haunt. She could poke around happily and see what was there before the sale.

There were no shoes on sale that day. It was mainly furniture and other household items. Some had obviously come from clearing out a house's contents — and it was nostalgic. Looking at the piles of crockery: plates, cups and saucers, and an old soup tureen.

The worn bone-handled cutlery, well used kitchen knives that the family had used for years. Then the dressing table's silver-backed brush, a faded photograph, and scent bottle, and she wondered what the person who'd owned them was like.

Then Katherine began to wonder what kind of a person Mrs Holt was. Now that she'd steeled herself to visit. What was her house like? Martin had said very little about his mother, except that Martin cared for her — and she liked to organise things. So Katherine imagined Mrs Holt's house would be very tidy — and her garden too.

Amongst the things she was looking at, something caught her eye. It was a shoe shaped flower pot!

It was a Dutch clog shape. White, with blue painted flowers on it. It was, Katherine thought, charming. And far from a price she could afford, she suspected.

The sale was beginning and as Katherine still had an hour before lunch, she decided to wait and see what the shoe-shaped flower pot fetched in the auction.

'Lot number one,' called the auctioneer. The bidding was brisk, and items were snapped up by those willing to buy.

Katherine found the selling interesting, and the auctioneer, she knew having bought second hand shoes there for years, was a lively character who always had a smile for the young nurse.

Some of the items were snapped up quickly, others the auctioneer tried to encourage someone to buy calling, 'Come on,' to the audience, and 'Any advance on one hundred pounds?' until the likely buyers shook their heads.

'Going, going, gone!' The auctioneer accepted the highest price he could get, then banged his little hammer down on his desk to make the deal final.

It was fascinating watching how high some prices went. Things Katherine admired were sold for far higher prices than she would have offered for them. And others would not sell, although the auctioneer was persuasive, urging them to take the items.

It was when she heard the words, 'Lot four-zero-four. Here I have a curio.

A shoe-shaped flower pot,' that Katherine pricked up her ears.

'I'll start at five shillings.'

No-one in the room responded.

'Four shillings?'

A cough by someone in the show-room made Katherine turn to look quickly at a gentleman in the front, but he waved his auction list to show he was not interested.

'A bargain for two shillings?'

What made Katherine bid she wasn't sure, except she suddenly thought it a pity such a pretty pot was not wanted. And what a lovely gift it would be for Martin's mother — she hoped — as she put up her hand and bought it.

★ ★ ★

Martin went home, as Sister had said, that afternoon, so Katherine didn't get the chance to see him again.

Her working week was hectic, but she found her life had become happier than she'd known it for some time. Back on the wards now that her arm was mended, she was engrossed in her new responsibilities as a third year nurse, and found it all very interesting.

Annette was working on the same ward too, so it was fun for them to be together, able to share the work and lift the spirits of the patients with pleasant chit chat.

Martin was always on Katherine's mind — she had to push thoughts of him aside when she needed to concentrate on her important job.

Annette teased her about Martin sometimes, saying, 'When is Jack the porter going to propose? Or are you engaged already?'

Wartime had made long engagements commonplace, and young people had to wait for years for their lover's return. Katherine knew she wanted to become qualified as a State Registered Nurse before she thought about marriage. So she said, 'Martin and I are not engaged. In fact, Annette, I doubt if we ever will be.'

'Why ever not?'

They were having a break and Katherine picked up her cup and took a sip of refreshing tea. 'Because of his mother.'

Annette's eyes bulged. 'His mother? What has she to do with it?'

Katherine took another sip of the hot tea. 'I'm sure I won't be good enough for his mother.'

Annette laughed. 'I don't believe that. Jack strikes me as being a man who would not be ruled by a woman. And as for his mother — you're not going to be marrying her — forget her.'

Katherine wished she could. She put down her cup, looked at her watch pinned to her dress, saying, 'Tomorrow at this time I'm going to be seeing Martin. He's staying at his mother's house while he is recovering from his accident, so I'll be seeing her too. Keep your fingers crossed I survive the ordeal.'

Annette laughed, 'She can't be that bad! Remember when we thought Matron was dreadful — but she's a treasure really.'

A Nervous Encounter

Katherine missed the first bus she could have taken to Wansford. That was because she'd got herself into such a state wondering what to wear, and then changing her mind at the last minute.

After washing and brushing her hair, she noted with satisfaction that it curled delightfully around her creamy neck. It was, she thought with satisfaction, a day when her hair was behaving well. It made up for her well worn blue dress, which was not fashionable.

Mrs Holt was bound to think Jilly Masters was better dressed. But she chose some pretty shoes from her collection to put on. They were her favourites and she hoped at least Martin would like them.

As she had the best part of half-an-hour to wait until the bus left for the village she decided she would pop into a florist and ask them to fill the little Dutch clog flower pot with a few flowers. Hoping it would make a better looking present for Martin's mother — even if she didn't like the shoe pot she might like the flowers.

When the bus came, and she was underway, she put the flower pot on the seat in front of her because there were very few people travelling on the bus midday, and began talking to a passenger who was keen to tell her all about her health problems.

Katherine listened politely but was pleased when the lady got off the bus. She had enough problems to face herself. Would she find she was still magnetically attracted to Martin — enough to be able to consider spending her life with him? That was, of course, if he asked her too. Would she be able to cope with his mother?

Was she imagining he loved her?

She had to find the answer to these questions, that was why she was going to see him — and his mother.

Wrapped up in her thoughts she was taken by surprise when she heard the conductor shout, 'Wansford!'

'Oh dear!' Katherine grabbed her handbag and rushed to get off the bus before it drove her back to Stamford.

The conductor gave her a knowing smile as she hopped off the bus saying, 'I thought I might have to come and wake you up, Miss. You looked as though you were in another world.'

'You're right, I was,' replied Katherine grinning at him.

It was only when she stood on the village bridge and saw the bus disappearing behind the hotel building she realised she'd forgotten the flower pot! She didn't have her present for Mrs Holt. What a shame!

She didn't have long to mourn the loss however, because there was Martin coming towards her on his crutches. With a dog on a lead.

Little Kim — because she was sure it was Kim — was behaving beautifully, not pulling or dancing about on his lead, which would make it difficult for Martin. The little dog trotted along waving his long-haired tail like a flag to welcome her.

It was Martin's friendly wave that dispelled her anxieties. But as he seemed anxious to get to her quickly, she called out in her nurse's voice, 'Steady on, Martin. You'll fall over if you try to run with your crutches.'

He slowed down a little, and his welcoming smile was delightful to see.

Walking nearer she began by saying, 'Sorry I missed the earlier bus — '

'Don't mention it. Kim and I need the exercise walking to the bus stop and back — although I did worry you had decided not to come.'

His concern that she might not have turned up melted her reserve and she said, 'Martin, surely you know I wouldn't let a good looking chap down?'

He laughed, 'I'm very glad to see you,' he came close to her and kissed her, making it seem as if he was truly overjoyed she'd come.

She was. It gladdened her heart to see both man and dog healing from their injuries.

'And I'm very pleased to see you,' she said becoming pink after hearing the warmth in his voice, and to hide her embarrassment she crouched down to stroke Kim.

Then to hide her intense feeling of joy at seeing Martin she said almost snappily, 'I had to see how my patient was progressing. Here, let me take the dog.'

'Very well,' he said giving her the lead and lifting both his crutches in the air and standing unaided.

'Don't do that,' she said, pretending to be cross. 'You'll fall over. And I can't pick you up.'

She could tell that he had not recovered as entirely as he seemed to think.

'Katherine, you have indeed picked my spirits up — I'm just so pleased to see you,' he said with unmistakable sincerity. And he bent to give her another quick kiss. It didn't seem to matter to him that they were exposed for anyone walking about the village to see.

'Martin, I think you had better go home, before you topple over.'

'Too late! I've already fallen — for you!'

She smiled fondly at him. And I for you, she thought.

They stood for a while in the middle of the old stone bridge, looking over at green meadows and down at the moving River Nene, dreaming their own thoughts and watching the smooth water pass under the arches, eddying around the tall grasses and rushes.

She felt him take her hand and she had no desire to release it.

It was a perfect time to enjoy the bliss of being in love, but reality soon crept in as he showed signs of needing to rest. Especially when a van rushed over the bridge and they had to squeeze close to the bridge wall.

'Martin,' she said, gently tugging his

hand, 'we can't stay here. You should sit down and rest that leg.'

'No, Nurse, we shouldn't!' He pretended to look serious. 'I have to start the potatoes boiling for lunch. Mother told me to put them on at half-past twelve and it's a quarter-to-one already.'

Katherine wondered why his mother didn't do it herself. Was Martin the houseboy?

'Come on, this way.' He indicated the road to take with his crutch. And Katherine gasped as he tottered. But he soon righted himself.

★ ★ ★

Reaching the house, she admired the lush, colourful flowers adorning the front garden. His mother was obviously an expert gardener. Katherine was glad she'd forgotten the flowers she'd intended to give to his mother. They would look very meagre — and his mother might even be insulted if she gave them to her.

He took out his key to open the door. 'After you,' he said, bowing her into the house.

Stepping into the hall, its cleanliness and airiness reminded her of the hospital's clean wards, and she felt more at home.

But she hadn't met his mother yet!

Martin said, 'Would you like to sit in the conservatory? It's nice and sunny in there, and there are some women's magazines to look at. I must get the vegetables on — or I'll be in trouble.'

Katherine said, 'If you don't mind, I'll come with you,' and followed him into the kitchen. She didn't want to be caught all alone by Mrs Holt.

The kitchen had sparklingly clean surfaces and Katherine thought Matron would approve. There was a cosy dog basket on the floor by the range, and Kim sank down in it looking out at her as if to say, this is my new home.

'Where's your mother?' she asked, wondering if the lady was upstairs.

'Oh, she went out to see a friend. She should be back soon.'

Katherine was used to helping her mum cook and after telling Martin to sit on a kitchen chair she began to take over the food preparation.

'I can't think what's happened to her,' Martin said, when the vegetables were cooked, 'but I know she would want us to eat and not wait for her.'

Katherine looked uneasy and Martin smiled at her reassuringly. 'Mum went to see a friend who has recently lost her husband. She's probably found she can't get away yet. She knows what it is like to be suddenly made a widow.'

Katherine immediately felt sympathetic. 'Did your father die recently?'

'Several months ago. But it's taking Mum a long time to adjust — my parents were very fond of each other. That's why I'm living here at present.'

Taking a deep breath in, Katherine felt she understood why Martin's mother seemed so possessive of her son. Just as her mother was of her, she supposed.

It made her see things in a different light. Mrs Holt was being kind visiting a friend in need. And if, as Martin said, she would like them to start the meal, then they should. She said, 'Shall I put your Mum's meal on a plate and put it in the oven to keep warm?'

'Good idea.'

The dining table was already laid, and Martin ate his casserole with relish.

'Don't you like your meal?' he asked, noticing her difficulty eating her it.

'Sorry, Martin, I don't feel very hungry.'

He looked at her plate. 'Well I'd better eat it then. Mother will be disappointed if she comes in and finds you can't stomach her cooking.'

'Martin, you know it's not the reason. There is nothing wrong with the meal. It's just that I, well . . . '

He looked at her keenly. Then he took her plate and scraped the food onto his.

'She asked me what she should cook for you,' he said. 'I had to admit I didn't know your likes and dislikes — so I said a casserole because I like them. Not a good choice for a summer day, was it?'

'I do like casseroles, Martin. And this one your mum made is delicious, but — '

He looked at her with concern, 'You're worried about something, aren't you?'

'Well,' she looked straight into his eyes deciding she should be honest with him, 'I have to admit . . . I'm afraid I may not get on with your mother.'

'Oh, you will,' he said confidently, as he finished eating and began to clear away the table.

Helping him with the dishes, she asked, 'How can you be so sure?'

'I told you before. She likes you.'

'I've never met her — so how can she know?'

Martin's voice sounded over the water gushing into the kettle ready to make coffee, 'Of course you've met her!'

Katherine's mouth opened to protest, and she frowned, puzzled. 'Was she a patient at the hospital?'

'No.'

Becoming a trifle annoyed with his calm insistence that they had met, Katherine asked sharply, 'Where then?'

'She told me she met you at the Auction Rooms in Stamford. Buying shoes.'

Katherine's eyes widened in amazement. 'You mean — she was the lady who bought me the miniature shoes?'

'I believe she did.'

Katherine was so overcome with relief that she found tears trickling down her face. After all the worry she'd had about meeting his mother for the first time, she now knew she couldn't have wished for a better outcome. Of course she remembered his mother — she was a darling!

He saw her sparkling eyes and came close to her. His large hand gently stoked her cheek. His thumb wiping away her tears. 'I had no idea you had been so worried about meeting her. I'm sorry, Katherine.'

'It's my mistake — ' she said feeling confused.

'Indeed not,' he said robustly. 'I understand now, it's my fault. I should explain. I know my mother was keen for me to marry Jilly Masters, and I think perhaps she led you to believe that we had gone away together for the weekend, which was untrue . . . Jilly and I have known each other since we were children. I like her, but only as a friend.'

Yes, Katherine had been distraught about thinking he might marry Jilly. A match encouraged by his mother. She feared he'd abandoned her — but she now understood why she had been misled.

Martin continued, 'It was unfortunate Mum didn't make it clear about me and Jilly — and told you who she was when you met her.'

'No, no,' cried Katherine, 'it was just one of those things. I admit I imagined

you and Jilly were more than friends
. . . and your mother and I just met by
chance. We talked together happily
about our shared interest in shoes, not
thinking about our names. Names are
not important — it is the person that
matters.'

'I agree. Whether you are called,
Katherine or Kitty, they are the same to
me.'

'As you are Jack, or Martin.'

They laughed.

'Let me explain. After your mother
kindly bought me the miniature shoes
she knew I liked, as a present, I
couldn't thank her because I didn't
know who she was.'

Martin listened, 'Well, you can thank
her now.' The dog was barking. 'Kim
can hear that she's just come in.'

Katherine stood up ready to greet
Mrs Holt, still reeling from the news.

What Katherine was amazed to see
was not just the lovely lady she'd
enjoyed coffee with after the sale, and
had given her the little shoes, but that

Martin's mother was carrying the Dutch clog flower pot she'd brought for her and left on the bus.

'Mum, meet Katherine. She's a shoe collector like you are.'

Katherine found no difficulty in greeting the kindly lady, whose pleasing features she remembered so well.

'How did you know I'd brought this for you?' Katherine asked looking at the distinctive flower pot.

'I saw it at the bus stop and the conductor told me a young lady had left it behind on one of the seats when she got off. So when he said she was a pretty girl with golden hair, I guessed it was Katherine — my future daughter in law. Hopefully.'

Martin protested. 'Mum! I haven't asked her yet to marry me, yet.'

'Well, it's about time you did!'

Embarrassed, Katherine changed the subject by saying, 'Your meal is keeping warm in the oven, Mrs Holt.'

'Do call me Valerie, dear.' She smiled fondly at the two young people. 'I'll eat my meal here in the kitchen,' she said. 'So you two can talk in the sitting room. I'll show Katherine my miniature shoe collection later.'

'I'm looking forward to seeing them,' Katherine said smiling.

'Mum likes to organise things,' said Martin as they left the kitchen and went into the sitting room where he lost no time in taking Katherine in his arms and they both enjoyed a prolonged kiss. 'Now we are alone,' Martin explained, 'it gives us time to sort out our future.'

'Have we anything to decide?'

'Mmm. I hope so. First of all — will you marry me?'

'Yes, I will,' said Katherine kissing him again with a singing heart. He'd not broken her heart a thousand ways, as the words of the popular song she often sang said — he'd only broken it once, and then mended it. Like a cobbler mended shoes.

No-one could be happier than Katherine to be in her shoes.

TAKE MY BREATH AWAY

Beth James

After the failure of her first marriage, romantic writer Emma has built a sheltered, secure life for herself and her four-year-old daughter. The last thing she needs on the horizon is a handsome stranger with an attractive smile. To make matters worse, her roof is leaking, money is tight and her ex-husband is taking a renewed interest in her life. Suddenly, Emma finds herself with as many complications to deal with as the tempestuous heroines in her romantic novels.

ALL ABOUT ADAM

Moyra Tarling

Teacher Paris Ford hopes to improve the performances of Brockton College's basketball team. But going to the new athletic director for help, she's confronted by the startlingly handsome Adam Kincaid. Years ago, Paris secretly witnessed Adam's role in her family's scandal and she isn't about to forgive or forget. However, Adam's tender kisses melt her resolve to maintain a professional relationship. Now she must discover the truth about Adam's past and look toward a future . . . with the man she loved.

NASHVILLE CINDERELLA

Julia Douglas

In Nashville, thousands of talented people hope to make the big time . . . Starstruck Cindy Coin came from Alabama, but still works in Lulu's diner, alongside Tony — who's yet to make his mark. Hank Donno, looking every inch the successful manager, hopes to find his big star — then wide-eyed Katie arrives. And travelling on the Greyhound, Texan Jack just hopes that Nashville is ready for him. Can hopes and dreams be realised? And is romance in the air in Nashville?

MY TRUE COMPANION

Sally Quilford

It is 1921. Social pariah Millie Woodridge is obliged to obtain employment as a companion for ageing actress, Mrs Oakengate, when her father is unjustly executed on charges of espionage. During a weekend house party Millie meets handsome adventurer, James Haxby, and is soon drawn into the dark, but thrilling world of espionage. Unsure who to trust, Millie joins James in tracking down a callous murderer and uncovering the truth about her father.

DATE DUE

926	R	85	
m'Bride			
m			
Pollock			

Demco, Inc. 38-293